Pledged

Loving Elizabeth Book 1

A Pride and Prejudice Novella Variation

Rose Fairbanks

Pledged
Published by Rose Fairbanks
©2018 Rose Fairbanks
ISBN-13: 978-1722638870
ISBN-10: 1722638877
Early drafts of this work were posted online.
All Rights Reserved. No part of this book may be reproduced in any form, except in the case of brief quotations embodied in critical articles or reviews, without permission in writing from its publisher and author.
Several passages in this novel are paraphrased from the works of Jane Austen.
This is a work of fiction. Any resemblance to characters, whether living or dead, is not the intention of this author.

Also by Rose Fairbanks

Jane Austen Inspired Fiction

The Gentleman's Impertinent Daughter
Letters from the Heart
Undone Business
No Cause to Repine
A Sense of Obligation
Love Lasts Longest
Once Upon a December
Mr. Darcy's Kindness
Sufficient Encouragement
Renewed Hope
Mr. Darcy's Bluestocking Bride
Extraordinary Devotion
Mr. Darcy's Miracle at Longbourn
Imagining Mr. Darcy
The Secrets of Pemberley

Paranormal Regency

Cinderella's Phantom Prince and Beauty's Mirror Anthology

Dedication

To my dear husband. They said we were too young and could not last. I am happier with you every day than the day before and could never imagine a more supportive and loving partner for my life. Here's to being crazy kids with you for another fourteen years!

Chapter One

June 20, 1806

"I would prefer to stay home this evening," Will Darcy grumbled.

"Are you such an old man now that an evening at the theatre is too much?" Will's older cousin, Captain Richard Fitzwilliam teased.

"Hardly," Will said dryly. He had just turned two and twenty. "Do not forget that you are older than me, Richard."

"All shall be well," Richard replied. "It is one evening out before a summer in Ireland with your friends." He motioned to their friends, Samuel Bennet and Charles Bingley. "You will be appearing with us, our sisters, and our fathers, not insipid debutantes and their matchmaking mamas. It is nothing compared to what the future will hold for you as the heir of Pemberley."

The young men had all met years ago at Eton and continued the friendship to their time at Cambridge. Along the way, they learned their fathers had been acquaintances during their youth. Inspired by their sons, the older generation soon took up a correspondence. The men had all met a few times over the years, but this was the first time that any of the ladies would be present.

Will, Sam, and Charles, all snorted and rolled their eyes simultaneously.

"You forget Louisa and Caroline will be there," Charles interjected.

"And though my mother is not present, rest assured she is scheming from afar," Sam concurred.

Will leaned back in his chair and groaned. "Richard, your mother gives me more pressure than anyone but Aunt Catherine!"

"Mother acts out of love, but let us be thankful she will not be present. Besides, your father has made it clear to Aunt that you are not to bend to her will."

"That is not the same thing as him believing I should choose my own bride." Will's shoulders slumped.

"Enough on Will's marital prospects. Sam, tell us about your sisters." Charles eagerly asked with his eyebrows raised in anticipation.

Sam grinned, "Now, Charles—and you, too, Richard—I know you cannot resist a pretty face but need I remind you, no idle flirtations with my sisters?"

"Now, come on man!" Richard gesticulated wildly. "Charles is too young, and I am too poor to take a wife. We would never trifle with a gentleman's daughter—especially a friend's sister. And Will here has never 'trifled' with anyone. We would only like to find ourselves in the company of beautiful women tonight."

Letting out an exasperated sigh, Sam continued, "Very well. Jane is quite beautiful. Blonde, blue-eyed, and willowy. She is charming and reserved in her expressions. She only sees the good in everyone, a veritable angel. Lizzy, though....she takes you by surprise. She is as dark as Jane is fair, and shorter too. She is outspoken and can even best my father in a debate. She might even be able to beat you, Will."

"A regular bluestocking, then?" Richard's eyebrows slanted down in disappointment.

"No, not at all. It is true she is well-read, but she is also witty and charming. She plays pianoforte very well, and her singing captivates audiences. Lizzy loves walking and enjoys nature. If it were not for the theatre and opera, or the museums and bookshops, she would never even come to town."

Charles' eyes grew wide, "She does not care to shop? Does not enjoy the balls and soirees? That is all Louisa and Caroline live for!"

"I doubt she is out yet. Is not she thirteen?" Will complained to hide his growing interest in the young lady. "Why are we speaking so much about a little girl? I am not going on and on about Georgie!"

Through the years of his friendship with Sam, Will had yet to meet Elizabeth but was impressed with what he knew of her. However, he had always thought of her as Sam's very young sister. Nothing could exist between them; even if he found her attractive and she was of courting age, she was his best friend's sister. If any of his friends ever fell in love with his sister, there would be pistols at dawn.

Sam shook his head. "Mary is thirteen. Lizzy is sixteen."

Will rolled his eyes, at sixteen she would still be a silly girl with little shape. He resisted the older, experienced widows that approached him at balls and did not partake of paid affairs but his celibacy did not blind him to the beauty of a grown woman's figure.

"She is out," Sam continued, "thanks to my stepmother. However, now that the entail is broken, I hope Mama can feel some relief." Sam shook his head and glared at Will. "We are speaking of her because she is a remarkable young lady and I was asked to share about her to three men who I trust. I think she could be a friend to you. Did I mention she can beat my father at chess?"

"Really?" Charles let out a low whistle. "Well, I daresay she is too much for me. I need a woman that is sweet, quiet, and level."

Winking at Charles and Richard, Sam baited Will. "Perhaps for you then, Richard?"

"She indeed sounds like a most extraordinary young lady. Will, you would have more time to bask in the attention of Bingley's sisters. What does she look like, Sam?" Richard leant forward as though eager to hear more.

"Yes," Will let out a derisive snort. "Since she has developed such a personality, she is probably merely tolerable and not handsome enough to tempt me at all."

"Tempt you!" Sam cried. "First of all, this is my sister! I would like her not to tempt anyone. What beauty holds you? You have criticised every beautiful woman of your acquaintance. Lizzy's personality could challenge and interest you. Her beauty will speak for itself." He paused and looked at his watch. "Enough teasing. I am thankful I can trust each of you with my sisters and need not fear you as potential suitors. Chaperoning them will turn me prematurely grey. Now, it is time to prepare for dinner; we had better get to it."

Will exited the library blushing at the description of himself, but he could not be sorry for it. *Is it too much to ask not to be bored by the woman I spend my life with? To enjoy her company at the end of the day instead of living separate lives? And be attracted to her as well?* However, he was only two and twenty and certainly had time to continue to look.

Let the horrible men find out about dinner some other way! Elizabeth thought as she returned to her bedchamber at Darcy House. She had been sent to remind her brother and his friends of the dinner hour. Instead, she overheard them talking about her and Will Darcy declaring her personality compensated for a lack of beauty. Her first reaction was to show the ungentlemanly young man his place and come down for dinner in a way that would make her mother proud. However, upon reflection she realised that she was not so vain as to care to show off like that, nor did she have such a gown with her at present. No, the gown she had planned to wear would service just nicely and what did she care if it earned his admiration.

Aside from the fact that he is the most handsome young man I have ever seen and has the most pleasing voice. Such thoughts brought back memories of what he said with such a voice. Spending too long in her musings, Elizabeth came down the stairs to overhear another conversation.

"I had sent Elizabeth to remind you all of the time, but you say that you did not see her? And she has yet to come down?" Mr. Bennet asked his son.

"Aye. I hope she is not ill," Sam replied.

"I doubt that. You know your sister's constitution. All the walking keeps her quite healthy."

"Oh, yes. We must not forget what a great walker Miss Eliza is," Caroline Bingley's sickly-sweet voice broke in.

She only met me this afternoon, and she acts as though she knows every intimate detail of my life!

Not caring for more abuse of herself, Elizabeth cheerfully called out from the open drawing room door. "Oh, I am here and quite well. I am afraid I merely lost track of time."

Ignoring the gentlemen, Elizabeth focused on her sister, Jane, in conversation with an amiable young man.

"Lizzy," Mr. Bennet called her attention away, "Sam told me that you never met him in the library. I know you cannot have forgotten where it is located. What happened?"

"Oh! Perhaps I am such a little girl that I could not be trusted with such a task?" She raised an eyebrow and resisted the urge to look at Fitzwilliam Darcy.

Mr. Bennet gave Elizabeth a puzzled look but shrugged. Muttering about not understanding the moods of ladies, he left the young people to their devices.

Richard inched closer to Elizabeth. "Sam, introduce us to your sister."

"My pleasure," Sam laughed, then performed the introductions of the two young men next to him.

Pledged

He continued to identify the occupants of the room. "Lizzy, you already met Miss Bingley and Miss Caroline. The gentleman mooning over Jane there is Mr. Charles Bingley. And the one talking with Father and Mr. Darcy is Charles's father, Mr. Joseph Bingley. Richard's father, Lord Fitzwilliam, and a few other relatives will meet us at the theatre."

Elizabeth gave them a dazzling smile that made her eyes sparkle. "Delighted to meet you."

Richard grinned in return. Elizabeth's words seemed to jolt Will to action, and he belatedly bowed. She turned her eyes on him, ready to tease him for his past words, but before she could say anything dinner was called. Richard offered her an arm to escort her to the table. Caroline and Louisa Bingley immediately seized Will's arms, claiming them for their own. Elizabeth inwardly laughed and wondered if the two sisters would fight over the pompous young man.

At the table, Elizabeth found herself situated near Will's father and easily made conversation with the older gentleman. "Mr. Darcy, I am very much looking forward to meeting Miss Darcy. Will she come downstairs this evening?" The Bennets had arrived during Georgiana's lessons, and due to her shyness, it was arranged for her to wait to meet the visitors.

"She will dine in the nursery, but will join us to exhibit on the pianoforte afterwards."

"Oh, dear Georgiana! How I long to see her again!" Caroline cried. "She is so talented on the pianoforte for such a young age. Yes, Miss Eliza, you must be quite dismayed to dine with us instead of with company better suited your age."

Caroline had just come out at the age of seventeen. Elizabeth internally rolled her eyes. Did Caroline dislike Elizabeth's age or did she see her as a threat for Will's attention? *She would find his opinion of me quite pleasing, I am sure.*

With good breeding, Elizabeth calmly ignored Caroline's comments. "I look forward to hearing Miss Darcy play later."

"And do you play as well, Miss Elizabeth?" Mr. Darcy asked.

"A very little and quite ill indeed."

"It is such a shame that we cannot all have access to the masters!" Caroline gave Elizabeth a pitying look. "However, I suppose the priorities of the country are quite different than Town."

"I cannot say for all of the country," Mr. Darcy spoke with a hint of irritation in his voice, "but it is true in Derbyshire. Miss Elizabeth, I am sure you are too modest. If it does not make you too uncomfortable, I ask you to play for us this evening."

Sam looked their way and gave his sister a puzzled look. "Lizzy plays quite well. I insist that you play for my friends."

"You are a very strange creature by way of brother!" Elizabeth laughed. "I would rather not play in front of those that must be used to hearing the very best. Yet, you know my courage always rises in the face of every attempt of intimidation."

"A theory as relevant for the drawing rooms of London as for his majesty's troops!" Proclaimed Richard and thus he turned Elizabeth's attention to himself for the remainder of the dinner.

Chapter Two

Will observed Elizabeth during the meal. Although trapped between the Miss Bingleys and unable to speak with his friend's sister, he recognised his father's look of approval. Elizabeth was shorter than average and, although Will was quite tall, he always had a soft spot for petite women. It brought out his protective instincts, and he could see that she could nestle under his chin nicely when embraced. During his mother's life, he had often seen his parents in just such a pose, and the image invoked all things comforting to him.

Although young, Elizabeth had a well-formed figure, with more curves than he would expect for her age. She had dark curly hair and eyes that quickly flashed from light hazel brown to a bright green. More than her physical attributes, something about her spirit attracted him. She could never be called small or ordinary.

Will's reverie ceased when his father decided to forego the usual separation of the sexes and invited everyone to the drawing room.

On their way, Richard drew closer to Will. Seeing his cousin's eyes follow Elizabeth, he clapped Will on the shoulder and whispered, "Bewitched yet?"

Will's eyes widened and he gulped but shrugged him off.

Mr. Darcy welcomed the ladies to sing and play. The Miss Bingleys eagerly displayed their abilities. Caroline had greater technical skill on the pianoforte, but Louisa was the better singer. When they were done, Sam reminded Elizabeth she was to play. She attempted to beg off, stating she was nothing compared to the other ladies, but her performance entranced Will. Although not superior to Caroline and Louisa's skill, Elizabeth played and sang with more emotion and obvious enjoyment.

Jane Bennet did not play or sing, but it hardly appeared to matter to Charles. Additionally, she seldom spoke. Will internally laughed at Charles's habit of falling for the prettiest girl in the room whether she had any sense in her head or not. At least Miss Bennet did not behave poorly or have a shrill voice. Some men had few requirements for what attracted them to the fairer sex. Will was not one of them.

Caroline played as her father sang in a rich baritone while Louisa turned pages, when

Georgiana came down at last. Mr. Bennet, Sam, and Elizabeth spoke amongst each other while Will's father and Richard laughed over something. Will sat alone. Georgiana's governess accompanied her, but the young girl gulped when she saw the number of people in the room.

"Papa..." The girl of twelve began.

Mr. Darcy looked up from his conversation. "Come along Poppet. Play us a new jig."

Georgiana looked around the room in distress. Will hated it when his father did this. Both Darcy siblings were shy and more like their mother, but their father could not understand their dispositions.

Will walked to his sister. "Georgie, if you play, then I will dance. You will be too busy laughing at your poor brother to feel nervous." She bit her bottom lip, and he continued, "Everyone present is certain to be pleased by your performance. I assure you, you will hear no unkind remarks."

At last, she nodded in acquiescence.

"Follow me," he whispered, and she placed her hand in his.

The others had stood when Georgiana entered the room, and everyone made the necessary bows and curtsies after Will performed introductions.

Mr. Darcy called Mr. Bennet and Sam over to him, leaving Elizabeth alone with the Darcy siblings.

Georgiana smoothed her hands over her skirts and remained mute until Elizabeth spoke.

"I am very pleased to meet you, Miss Darcy. I have heard you are very accomplished on the pianoforte."

Georgiana blushed. "Thank you, Miss Elizabeth, but I am too young to be very accomplished at anything. I am certain you must play better than me."

"Never assume age is a disadvantage...or an advantage. Most things in life are learned traits and not inherent abilities. I am told you practice very diligently, whereas I forsake my practice for other pursuits."

"Yes," Georgiana nodded. "Miss Graves tells me I play too much, and will never be a truly accomplished young lady if I do not also put effort into other tasks."

Elizabeth laughed. "Miss Graves is undoubtedly correct, but I did not mean that I am engaged in ladylike accomplishments." She gave Will a conspiratorial look before leaning in closer to Georgiana as though speaking in confidence. "I read everything I can get my hands on and I go on very long walks all over the countryside. I play chess with my father and delight in arguments, or as my mother would say 'vexing her.'

"I take no enjoyment in sewing, embroidery, drawing, painting tables, or netting purses. I have acquired only the basic skills for each. With four sisters our house will be overflowing with tables and fireplace screens in a year or so. If playing pleases you so much, why should you not be able to enjoy it?"

She then looked toward Will as though asking him to challenge her. Caroline Bingley approached before Will could reply to Elizabeth. The Bingleys had just finished their performance.

"Oh, Miss Darcy! How nice to see you again! How well you look! And my! You must have grown. Mr. Darcy, do you think she will be as tall as me?"

Caroline stood as close to Will as was decent. He supposed she was trying to display her height, believing he would desire a woman of her attributes. She did not allow him to comment.

"Well, do come Miss Darcy. I long to hear you play again! Now, I will turn your pages."

Caroline began to lead Georgiana to the instrument when the latter looked toward Will.

"Georgie will you play a reel? I would love to dance with so many fair partners."

Instantly, Caroline took a step closer to Will. Out of the corner of his eye, he saw Elizabeth turn her head to hide a smile.

"Miss Caroline," Elizabeth said. "I am not inclined to dance this evening. May I be of service to Miss Darcy so you might be available?"

Caroline readily agreed, and although Will knew it meant he would have to dance with Caroline instead of Elizabeth, he was pleased with the way she rescued his sister.

Soon the rug was rolled up, and Georgiana played lively Scottish tunes. Elizabeth turned the pages while the other young people danced. Caroline looked incredibly smug, at first, until Will began to make some faces and dance badly, earning giggles from his sister. Before too long, another gentleman entered the room.

"George! How are you, my boy?" Mr. Darcy exclaimed. He quickly introduced George Wickham, his godson and steward's son to the room. "George, I must see you dancing with the other young people."

"I would be delighted to, Mr. Darcy," Wickham flashed a smile, "but it seems all the young ladies have partners."

"Nonsense, Miss Graves can dance with you."

"Miss Graves?"

"Oh, you have not been introduced yet!" Mr. Darcy directed Wickham to the twenty-something lady sitting in a chair near the pianoforte and watching her charge. "George Wickham, meet Miss Laura Graves. She is Georgiana's new governess."

Will could easily tell Wickham found Miss Graves attractive. Although not a great beauty, she looked pretty enough. Wickham preyed on servant women who either easily succumbed to his charms, or were too embarrassed to confess anything to their masters. This was the only reason Will could believe it a good thing Wickham was to leave with the other gentlemen in a few days.

Wickham gave her an impeccable bow. "Miss Graves, would you care to dance?"

"Oh, I had not thought to dance this evening."

Will heard her voice waver and wondered if the housekeeper had forewarned her of Wickham. Mr. Darcy frowned at her response and Will intervened. While Georgiana and Elizabeth selected the next piece, the room grew quiet. Conscious that they could all hear his conversation, he nevertheless persisted. "Miss

Graves, might you allow Miss Elizabeth a respite from her duties? Or perhaps you might play, and Georgiana could rest?"

Mr. Darcy broke in, speaking in a firm tone. "It is good for Georgie to practice and she does not need help to turn the pages for one last jig. Now, I insist all the young people dance."

Miss Graves paled a little and Will wondered if she might beg off and claim to be ill, but he chose to try again. "Then, I insist your first dance of the night be with me." Will ignored the raised eyebrows of many people in the room as he led her to the dance floor.

While Caroline let out an audible huff, Will made quick eye contact with his friends, and a wordless scheme was put in place.

Caroline paired with Richard, Charles stayed with Jane, Sam partnered with Elizabeth, leaving Wickham with Louisa Bingley. The gentleman had earlier pieced together the likelihood of Wickham appearing and how they would safeguard the ladies. They believed the Bingley sisters the least likely to be susceptible to his charms as they valued wealth and connections over ideas of romance.

The four friends had focused on protection and not fairness or sensibilities. Belatedly, Will realised he made Miss Graves break propriety by dancing with him after refusing Wickham. Additionally, Elizabeth looked displeased with her brother as a partner. Her eyes continued to seek out Wickham, who she undoubtedly saw only as a handsome and agreeable young man. Will and the others continued to block Wickham's attempts at speaking with Miss Graves. As the night wore on, his expression turned stony.

The following day, Elizabeth arose early. Always an earlier riser, she slept restlessly in unfamiliar beds and homes. Additionally, the events of the evening before circled in her mind. Why should Sam's friend be so rude to Mr. Wickham? Mr. Darcy had been the only one friendly to Wickham. The old man's son and his friends believed they knew better than the patriarch. Elizabeth shook her head at such disrespect.

Her father had always inspired deep respect in her. Her mother on the other hand… Elizabeth frowned. It was not that she desired to disrespect her mother. The woman merely had such different understanding and feelings of all the world than Elizabeth. When she was younger, she thought perhaps it was because Fanny Bennet was her step-mother, but Elizabeth now saw the same disconnection in temperaments between Fanny's eldest daughter and the woman. Fanny's daughter, Mary, was much more severe and studious than the youngest Bennet daughters. Their frivolity and love of luxuries bordered on spoilt. When Elizabeth would mention as much to her father or brother, they would laugh. Why should they moderate their spending when Sam was breaking the entail? When the sad day came that Mr. Bennet died, Sam would become master. All of his sisters and step-mother would forever be welcome at Longbourn. Additionally, Sam's betrothed was the daughter of the local knight and Elizabeth's close friend. Charlotte would never toss them in the hedgerows.

Yes, as much as Elizabeth respected and loved her father, she had to admit he was just a little blind when it came to the ways of his second wife. However, Elizabeth would never publicly argue with either one of her parents or disrespect their requests as Fitzwilliam Darcy had done. On the other hand, even Sam seemed to agree with his friend. Could Sam be so easily led astray?

Elizabeth quietly dressed for the day, although she knew Jane would still be asleep. Perhaps all the extra rest was what made Jane so beautiful. Of course, all the slumber in the world could not change Elizabeth's disposition. Jane was mild and sweet-tempered whereas Elizabeth delighted in sarcasm and debates. Some, like Louisa and Caroline Bingley, would call her unladylike. Elizabeth shrugged as she ran a brush through her brown tresses. She cared not one jot for the opinion of those ladies.

With silent steps, Elizabeth crossed the spacious chamber and softly shut the door behind her. The Darcys' enormous London house had none of the old squeaks and groans of Longbourn. The stairs made no complaint as she descended them in favour of the Library. Pausing outside the door, Elizabeth listened for voices, hoping the room was empty. Satisfied there were no occupants, Elizabeth eased the door open and sighed at the glorious sight of so many rows of books. Undoubtedly the work of several generations, Elizabeth could not help but admire the dedication it took to amass such a stockpile of tomes.

Running her fingers over the woodgrain of the cases, Elizabeth noticed a partially hidden notch. Touching it, she felt the wood push in a little and heard a soft click. A panel on the edge of the case by a door that opened to Mr. Darcy's dressing room eased open. Curious, Elizabeth approached and peered in the empty hidden cupboard. Suddenly, she heard a sound coming from the dressing room. Panicking, Elizabeth slid inside the closet and pulled the panel closed.

"Enough, Fitzwilliam," Mr. Darcy said. "George will accompany us. This childish rivalry you have needs to come to an end. One day you will be master of Pemberley and George will be there to help you just as his father has assisted me."

"I have the highest respect for Mr. Wickham, Father. As your steward, I agree he has been indispensable to you, but his son..."

"Will," Mr. Darcy sighed. "Sometimes I see too much of your mother's pride in you. Perhaps we ought not to have named you after her side of the family. They can be so exclusive with their lofty titles."

"I am sorry you think so."

Elizabeth believed it was said with a mixture of offense and regret.

"I finalized everything yesterday. He will have the living at Kympton. After this summer, he will begin his training to be rector, and you will begin learning more about Pemberley. Together, you will be the models all of Derbyshire gentry class will aspire to be."

"Yes, sir," Will said. "Ah, here is the Plato I wanted."

"Now, let us find breakfast. Bennet and Sam ought to be down any moment. Undoubtedly the ladies will sleep until later. Will you join us at the club?"

They exited through the library door and left for the breakfast room, Elizabeth assumed. Her mind whirled with all she had heard. Even Will's father called him proud! Elizabeth lingered in the library until she heard voices on the stairs. Hearing her father's voice, she met him and both Mr. Bingleys in the hall.

"Lizzy," Papa said and kissed her cheek. "I trust you are well."

"Indeed," Elizabeth smiled. After greeting the others, she placed her hand on his arm, and they walked to the breakfast room together.

"Have you been in the library long?" Mr. Bennet asked as they entered the room.

Mr. Darcy and Will stood and bowed at her entrance, but the younger man's eyes met hers with a curious gaze.

"No, only for a moment," she answered and fought a flush coming to her cheeks. "I must have just missed you upstairs."

Mr. Bennet chuckled. "And, of course, you thought of reading before food."

Mr. Darcy smiled. "My son is also a great reader, Miss Elizabeth."

"I wish I could take that term as a compliment, but my mother assures me it is a very troublesome habit," Elizabeth said with a sly smile.

The gentlemen laughed.

"I am sure she would," Mr. Darcy said with a grin.

"What sort of books do you enjoy reading?" Will asked.

"Whatever captures my imagination," she shrugged.

"Novels," Will supplied.

Perceiving his disapproval, Elizabeth drew her shoulders back. "I do appreciate novels, but I read many things. Poetry, engineering, history—surely that calls for as much imagination as anything with the way the writers have imagined the thoughts and words of the world's greatest men and women." She raised a brow. "I even find enjoyment in philosophical treatises such as The Republic."

Will's mouth dropped open before he managed to speak. "You read Plato?"

"In the Greek," Mr. Bennet grinned. "Sam taught her. They drive my wife mad with speaking in 'foreign tongues' as she calls it."

"Telling of my exploits, Father?" Sam said from the doorway. With a bow to its occupants, he took a seat next to his friends.

"There would be nothing to tell," Elizabeth shook her head. "You are the very best brother and the most gentlemanly man. Papa is far more likely to find stories to tell of me."

Sam raised his brows and then looked between the gentlemen before they all burst out in laughter. Elizabeth blushed in embarrassment.

"Never mind us, Miss Elizabeth," Will said when they had calmed. "We see a different side of your brother than perhaps you do, but I would hope one day my own sister may say the same of me."

"Surely she will," Mr. Darcy cut in. "Fitzwilliam knows the Darcy legacy he must live up to. He has always made me proud, and I know he will never disappoint me."

As the older man spoke, Elizabeth thought she saw Will's previous amusement fade. Such words ought to inspire well-deserved pride and affection. Instead, Will looked a bit like a man trying not to choke.

"Well, what are the plans for the morning?" Mr. Bingley asked.

"I invited Fitzwilliam and his friends to the club, but he has declined. I suppose the young people would prefer to find other forms of amusement."

Sam nodded. "Yesterday, Charles said his sisters wanted to walk in the park during the fashionable hour and then visit a few shops."

"Very good," Mr. Darcy smiled at his guest. "I expect you and Fitzwilliam will accompany the ladies."

Elizabeth saw the nearly imperceptible set of Will's jaw tighten. Meeting his father's eyes, he nodded. Next, he met Elizabeth's gaze. Her breath stole as she thought she could read the young man's feelings and found they reflected her own. Fitzwilliam Darcy was a puzzle she seemed in no danger of solving anytime soon.

Chapter Three

Following breakfast, the young people gathered in the drawing room. Jane came downstairs just before the Bingleys arrived. Despite Caroline and Louisa suggesting the day before they meet for their outing at eleven, they did not reach Darcy House until half past the hour. Will rolled his eyes. They claimed they did not want to seem too eager and miss the greatest of personages to be seen during the fashionable hour in Hyde Park. Fortunately, the Bennet sisters seemed entirely unaffected by the notion.

Charles seized the first opportunity to speak with Jane and offered himself as an escort. Although Elizabeth had been down the entire time, Will had finally screwed up enough courage to ask to be her escort. Before he could ask, however, Charles' detested sisters plastered themselves to Will's side. Once again, Elizabeth was left with Sam as company. As much as she appeared to like her brother, Will would guess most young ladies would want more attention from other males.

Caroline and Louisa chirped nonsense in his ear all the while he attempted to listen to Sam and Elizabeth's conversation behind him. They greeted many acquaintances on the path and Will was pleased to see the pride in which Sam introduced his sisters. They appeared welcoming but modest, whereas Charles' sisters always acted as though they expected more praise from their brother and instant fawning from whoever they met. It was no different when Lord Harcourt approached them.

Harcourt had attended Eton and Cambridge the same years as Will and Sam but their careers as students diverted there. Harcourt embraced the tyrannical lifestyle favoured by some boys as a way of exerting some semblance of power and authority over others. Wickham soon became acquainted with Harcourt and his ilk. Will barely contained his surprise when the young earl stopped Sam by name.

"Bennet, we are overdue a conversation, are we not?" Harcourt drawled, stopping their entire party.

Will raised his brows at his friend, who did not signal back he needed assistance.

"And who do we have here?" the Lord smiled at Elizabeth and then examined her head to toe the way he would his nightly courtesan.

Will watched as Sam pulled Elizabeth slightly closer and covered her hand with his. "My sister, Miss Elizabeth Bennet. Lizzy, meet Lord Harcourt."

"My lord," Elizabeth curtseyed.

"You have not been in London before, have you? I would recall you."

His words were beyond impertinent and Will noted he did not confine himself to a more acceptable, although still too forward in his imagination, compliment of saying he would recall her face.

"I have only been to visit my aunt and uncle, my lord."

"Yes, this is Eliza's first time out in Society," Caroline pushed forward then cleared her throat.

Bingley sighed. "My younger sister Caroline and my elder sister Louisa. Girls, as you heard, Lord Harcourt."

"That would be the Seventh Earl of Harcourt, correct?" Caroline asked.

"Indeed." Harcourt looked bored as the sisters attempted to rein in their enthusiasm. His interest returned to Elizabeth, and he eyed her with unconcealed lust.

"And on Bingley's arm is one of my other sisters, Jane," Sam said.

Harcourt barely spared her a glance and Elizabeth began to shrink from his gaze. Her cheeks were red, and she stared at her feet.

"Come, no need to be shy," Harcourt said and moved forward.

Primal jealousy stirred in Will's chest, and he had to contain a growl.

"We will soon be excellent friends, I am sure."

"My lord?" Elizabeth lifted her face, confusion in her eyes.

"I believe you wished to speak with me, my lord," Sam said. "Darcy and Bingley, would you continue to escort the ladies?"

Caroline stammered out that she wished to remain and Louisa echoed her.

"Perhaps we might wait while you discuss whatever your business is a few steps away," Charles suggested.

Harcourt shrugged, and Sam led him several feet away.

Will shook his head. He did not like how Harcourt continued to eye Elizabeth. "Come, Miss Elizabeth. I believe you would enjoy continuing forward," he offered his arm.

Elizabeth hesitated but placed her hand around his arm. Will thought he felt a slight tremor.

"Are you well?" he asked once they were away from the others.

"That man...I do not trust him." A shudder racked her frame.

"You are correct not to trust him."

"What has he done?"

"I should not say," Will answered. "I wish I could warn every man and woman in creation."

"Is he so wicked?"

"He is among the worst of men, but I do not wish to speak of such things."

"Do you think it distresses me?" Elizabeth let go of Darcy's arm and paused to look at a specific visage.

"I would not do you the dishonour. I am merely loathe to talk about such a reprobate before a beautiful young lady."

Elizabeth smirked. "Oh, you have charming words when alone with a young lady, but before your peers, you must malign the same lady sight unseen."

"Based on your behaviour last night, I had thought you heard. Pray, forgive me and allow me to thank you for not displaying my shame to my friends and father."

Elizabeth turned to face him, her head cocked to one side, as she considered his request. "Very well, I do forgive you. Only flattery is not necessary. Thank you for relieving me of the discomfort of Lord Harcourt's company."

Elizabeth returned to Will's side but did not take his arm, he noted with irrational longing. They resumed walking. "No thanks is necessary, nor did I flatter you."

Elizabeth laughed. "Oh, I know I am not the beautiful sister. Fortunately, my vanity has never taken that turn. I would much rather be thought clever and allow my dear Jane to have all the admiring beaus."

Will lightly gripped Elizabeth's wrist, staying her movements. "Your sister is lovely, but it was your eyes that captivated me last night."

Elizabeth's mouth hung open in an O. She looked so adorable Will felt the need to continue.

"Your smile sets my heart racing, and your voice enthralls me. Your wit and sharp mind have my admiration while making me inwardly chuckle. Your face or figure alone might not meet Society's definition of beauty but you are beautiful, and I am pleased to have your individual attention."

Elizabeth blushed flame red, but she did not look uncomfortable as she did under Harcourt's gaze. She met Will's eyes, as though attempting to assess if he meant his words. She seemed at a loss of what to say.

"Shall we continue?" Will again offered his arm and this time, Elizabeth took it.

They ambled along for some time comparing the differences between Hertfordshire and Derbyshire countryside. Suddenly, Elizabeth recognized their surroundings. They had long left the fashionable path and scarcely met a passerby.

"I know this area," Elizabeth grinned. "I come here with my aunt and uncle and their children. The little ones delight in feeding the ducks."

Another bend in the path displayed a small brook and a few children gathered near with a governess or nursemaid. Elizabeth approached one. "Can you share with my friend and me?"

The child held out a sack and Elizabeth reached her hands, pulling pulled out fistfuls of breadcrumbs. "Here," she thrust some into Will's hands.

"What am I supposed to do?" He asked, loving the amusement in Elizabeth's eyes. Caroline was right in a way. There was a sort of youthful exuberance around Elizabeth, but she was not child-like.

"You toss the crumbs out like so." Elizabeth scattered a few pieces on the ground and ducks waddled over, quacking along the way. The children clapped and giggled.

"This is entertaining?" Will frowned and repeated her motions.

"I suppose you would rather be shooting at them with a gun," Elizabeth murmured.

"I do enjoy hunting," Will confessed, "but less for the sport than for the opportunity to be outdoors."

"And such this is for children," Elizabeth nodded.

"And young ladies?"

"Some ladies, of all ages, I imagine," Elizabeth blushed.

"My mother used to put bird feeders up around the gardens of Pemberley," Will confessed. "I did not mean to criticise."

"It is not so different," Elizabeth agreed. "My sisters and I do the same at Longbourn. When in London, I am often inside and find it so stifling. A long walk in the park is just what I need. This corner is rather distant from the rest of the park, and so it is a favourite."

Will looked around. It was rather distant from where they began. "We should return. The others will be wondering where we are and they had wanted to go shopping."

"Oh, by the time we meet them it will be too late to go shopping at any rate. We may as well enjoy ourselves here and allow them to go without us."

"How sly you are, Miss Elizabeth!" Will chuckled. She had neatly placed them in a position where they had the perfect excuse for missing the tedious part of the morning. "You do not wish to go shopping?"

Elizabeth shrugged. "I certainly do not want to go shopping with the Miss Bingleys."

"What shall we do instead?" Will asked as he guided her to a nearby bench.

"Tell me about Scotland and Ireland. Have you visited your estates there before?"

"Yes, a few times when my mother was alive but not since. I fear my memories would be through the eyes of a child."

"And does that make them less valuable? Do you think a child recognizes the fields as any less green or the seaside as less magnificent?"

"The opposite, I am sure," Will said with a growing smile. "Very well."

As Will launched into descriptions from his childhood memories of far-flung places, several more families with children came and went. Some of them fearlessly approached Elizabeth. A few she seemed to be on friendly terms with, complimenting them on how much they had grown since last year and speaking with whoever chaperoned them. They all invited her to play with them. She encouraged the fearful ones and cautioned the adventurous ones. She chased and laughed as the children squealed with joy.

Will watched with a growing warmth spreading in his chest. Hours ago, they had left the high society of London behind, and he had never been happier. He did not care for the balls of the haute ton and the matchmaking mamas or money hungry debutantes. When he considered what he desired in the future, it was what these families had. A brood of happy children, living far away from the harshness of city life. Of course, a man did not make such a blissful family on his own, and he began to think he had met the companion he desired by his side.

"Where did you get to, Lizzy?" Jane asked when Elizabeth arrived in at Darcy House with windblown hair and rosy cheeks.

Elizabeth rushed to her chamber and asked for Jane's help in dressing for the theatre. "We walked too far and lost track of time. When we realised how long we had been gone, we also noted you all would have already left for shopping. Did you enjoy yourselves?"

Jane beamed. "We did! Mr. Charles talked with me the entire time. We chatted about the weather and the condition of the roads. He is so amiable! The Miss Bingleys—Caroline and Louisa as they have asked me to call them—were kind enough to show me the most fashionable jewellery. I had thought they were too expensive, but Sam said no. In the end, he chose a surprise for both of us."

Elizabeth's head popped up at Jane's last words. She had been attempting to conceal sly smiles at her sister's description of the day. Of course, Jane limited herself to discourse with

Charles about the most inane topics, but they both found the other charming. Equally predictable was his sisters' suggestion of ostentatious accessories. What Elizabeth could not credit was Sam buying them fine jewellery. A knock on the door interrupted her musings.

"Tie me up, Jane," Elizabeth came to her sister's side. "Just a moment!" she called out to the person on the other side of the door.

"It is I, your anonymous gift-bearer," Sam said theatrically from the other side of the wood panel.

"You may enter," Elizabeth grinned when Jane had finished lacing the back of her gown.

"Ah, just as I thought. Jane in the blue and Lizzy in the yellow. I believe you will find the following pieces go with your attire." Sam held out two boxes.

Jane and Elizabeth shared a smile before opening their treasures. Elizabeth gasped at hers. Sam had given her a necklace, bracelet, and earring set of amber and pearls. The necklace had a heavy amber pendant at the centre then alternated with small ambers and larger pearls. The bracelet was silver around amber and mother of pearl, both in ovals. Simple earrings of round amber and teardrop pearls finished the set. Looking at Jane's, Elizabeth marvelled again. A unique necklace of sapphires arranged like feathers with silver filigree made the collection unique and stunning. Sapphires and diamonds adorned the bracelet and earrings.

"Sam, how ever did you afford this?" Elizabeth gasped. "Two sets of jewellery en suite!"

"I have saved wisely, my dear sister," Sam tweaked Elizabeth's nose before assisting her with the necklace clasp. "Additionally, I have made wise investments."

"You have?" Elizabeth had never heard him mention them before. She swiftly rearranged her hair with some jewelled combs.

"Come, would you not rather enjoy an evening at the theatre and in one of the best boxes than listen to your older brother go on about boring investments?" He held out his arms for his sisters to grasp.

Elizabeth nodded and joined his side. They left the chamber, and she hesitated just before they descended the stairs. "I was so rushed; I worry I will look a disgrace."

"You are lovely, Lizzy," Sam said and kissed her on the cheek.

Elizabeth smoothed her gloved hand over her gown of amber crape over white sarsenet. Trimmed with pearls, it created a belt around her natural waist, and an added ruffle gave her hips more dimension. Elizabeth was of the mind that she should not fight her natural shape for the sake of fashion. She did not have Jane's willowy figure. Instead, she chose gowns which could emphasize her curves. About halfway down the stairs, others gathered in the entry. Among them, Will. He looked up, and Elizabeth saw his jaw drop before his eyes scanned her body. They met hers, and although a smile did not form on his lips, Elizabeth saw one in his eyes all the same. They shined in admiration, causing Elizabeth's heart to pound.

They had no time to converse. The Bennets loaded into their carriage, the Bingleys and Darcys in their own conveyances. At the theatre, Mr. Bennet escorted Jane, and Elizabeth entered on Sam's arm. Arriving with the Darcys drew the notice of most of the crowd, and it amused Elizabeth how so many scowled in her direction. She smiled back. Of course, Caroline Bingley matched the nasty looks. Caroline had also worn an amber gown with a natural waist, and she fumed in Elizabeth's direction every chance she got. When Elizabeth had seen the strange oblong cutouts across Caroline's bosom, exposing the white satin slip, she broke into laughter and feigned a coughing fit to conceal it.

Now, she followed as Sam led them to the Darcy theatre box. She sat on the end, next to her brother, and soon her attention was captured by the actors on stage. During the break, an unwelcome figure emerged from the shadows outside the box.

"Miss Elizabeth Bennet, I thought I saw you," Lord Harcourt said and bowed over her hand, bringing it to his lips.

"My lord," Elizabeth mumbled and attempted to pry her hand from him.

"Harcourt," Sam said with a frown. Mr. Bennet called out to him. "Pardon me, I will be but a moment."

After Sam had left, Harcourt grinned at Elizabeth. "What lovely jewels you wear this evening, madam," Harcourt ran his fingers below the line of Elizabeth's necklace.

Bile rose in her throat, and she held her breath until he removed his digits.

"I believe you asked for refreshment," Will said from over Elizabeth's shoulder. "If you will excuse us, Harcourt." He held out his hand for Elizabeth to take.

"Harcourt, is that you, man?" Mr. Darcy asked and held a small quizzing glass to his eye.

"Good sir," Harcourt nodded then returned his eyes to Sam as he returned to them.

"Miss Elizabeth," Will said and tugged on her hand.

Elizabeth stood to leave with Will but just before going heard Harcourt speak with her brother.

"You have already spent the money, I see. Do not forget what you owe me!"

Sam looked defiantly at the bully, but Elizabeth could not hear his reply before they left the box.

"Why does Lord Harcourt need to speak with my brother again?" Elizabeth attempted to slow Will's long strides which pulled them further away from the box. "He said something about money. Has my brother borrowed money from him?"

Will finally ceased walking and pulled them to a quiet corner. "I do not know, but I would caution you against speaking so openly about finances or Harcourt."

Elizabeth's mouth dropped open. "Oh, I had not considered the other people..."

"Think nothing of it. London is far larger than your market town. Even when you think you are having a private conversation, there is always someone nearby who might hear. By the same token, there are so many people most people are ignored."

"Is that where you learned it from?"

"Learned what?"

"Ignoring others. Seeming to find others invisible."

Will blinked at her. "I do not consciously ignore others. My mind is often preoccupied with matters that do not concern those around me."

Cocking her head to one side, Elizabeth determined Will sincerely meant his words. "I suppose that is true. You are not above insults when you dislike someone."

"Are you never going to let me forget that?"

From the corner of her eye, Elizabeth could see Will's smirk.

"I said I forgave you, not that I could forget it. Such harsh words on such a fragile mind can wreak havoc." Elizabeth feigned a dramatic pose, and Will chuckled.

"I would have been an even bigger idiot if I had said your mind was weak. I had not known you more than a minute before perceiving the liveliness of your mind."

"Is that what you thought of me when you first saw me?"

Will shook his head. "Your beauty stunned me into silence." He cast a long look over her. "Much like it did tonight."

Elizabeth smiled at his praise before allowing it to fall and wrinkling her brow.

"What is it?" Will asked and took a step closer.

"I do not want to return to the box if he is there. I cannot abide…" Elizabeth paled and began to shiver.

Will pulled them deeper into the recess of the hallway. He rubbed his hands up and down her arms to warm her. "You are safe. No matter what Sam's business is with Harcourt, I know on my life that he would never knowingly endanger any of his family. While you are in London, Sam has tasked his friends with watching over you and your sister."

"Is that why you are spending so much time with me?" Elizabeth hated the thought that Will might think her in such need of protection or view her as an obligation.

Will sighed. "That should be the answer I give you, but I hate deceit. The truth is, I always wish to be in your company. When Harcourt touched you..."

He trailed off, but Elizabeth saw how Will clenched his fists at his side.

"I did not say thank you earlier," Elizabeth seized on Will's latter statement. "It is not because I am ungrateful or discourteous. Rather, I lacked the courage to reference the incident. I did notice how quickly you came to my aid. Now, please accept my thanks."

"I cannot," Will shook his head. "I thought only of you and your safety. I had no intentions of doing anything heroic. I neither confronted nor fought him. My only aim was to get you to safety. I do not want your thanks."

Elizabeth bit her lip before looking up at Will through her lashes. His eyes were fixed on her face. "What do you want from me then?"

Will's eyes widened, and a low groan rippled down his throat. He squeezed his mouth shut tightly before returning to his indifferent expression. Something about the return of his lips on his face caused Elizabeth to stare. She had never considered a gentleman's lips before.

"We should return to the box. I am certain Harcourt is gone. I saw him walk past a few moments ago."

"Oh. Then why did you not escort me back already?"

"Why should I share you when I can have you all to myself here?"

Elizabeth blushed. "Is that is what you want? I shall be your secret theatre sweetheart?"

"No," Will answered, and his jaw momentarily tightened. A grim expression crossed his face. "That is not what I would want, but I fear none would be happy to see my admiration for you."

"Why is that?" Elizabeth frowned.

"That is too complicated to explain at the moment." Will sighed. "And pointless to discuss. We must return, now."

Elizabeth said nothing as Will directed them back to the box, but his words echoed in her mind for the remainder of the evening. Why would their friends and family dislike their attachment? And why should it not be discussed between them?

Chapter Four

As Will escorted Elizabeth back to the box, he was approached by several gentlemen. Some were fathers thrusting their daughters before him. Others were brothers attempting to unburden themselves the task of chaperoning a proper lady. Undoubtedly, in the interest of spending more time with the merry widows and the courtesans who frequented the theatre. All looked at Elizabeth with disdain, and very few asked for any introduction at all. The expressions of displeasure from the gentlemen were nothing compared to the scorn from the ladies.

Surprisingly, Elizabeth held her own. She returned jealousy with kindness, finding something to say to each lady who deigned to speak with her. Just before they reached the box, Will whispered to her.

"That is a very interesting and provocative smirk you are wearing Miss Bennet."

"Is it?" Elizabeth's smirk grew to a grin.

"Will you tell me what amuses you? Is it how you met with all those people with such equanimity?"

"Why should I worry for their approval or disapproval? I am the lady on the arm of Fitzwilliam Darcy. Their spiteful acts of jealousy did all the work of proving me the greater lady without my having to put forward any effort at all. Yes, I am quite pleased with the trouble they saved me."

Will smiled as well until he saw Sam and a familiar but unwelcome figure from the corner of his eye. Reaching the box, he urged Elizabeth forward. "I will just be a moment."

After she entered behind the curtain, Will moved to where Sam stood in the shadows arguing with the woman who was supposed to be his former mistress.

"Sam, Miss Johnson, I hope I am not interrupting anything."

"Lucy was just leaving," Sam said with raised brows.

"Yes, pardon me," Miss Lucinda Johnson nodded. "I tire too easily these days to enjoy a performance at the theatre. Good evening, Mr. Darcy. It was a pleasure to see you again. Sam..." She trailed off and then her eyes filled with tears. Miss Johnson cleared her throat then left without a backward glance.

"Sam—"

"I know. I know," Sam cut off Will's words. "It is not fair to Charlotte."

"No, it is not. You entered a betrothal with Miss Lucas and swore to give up Lucy."

"I did," Sam agreed. "However, denying my heart is not fair either."

"It is too late for that now. You ought to have thought better before you proposed. I know you would never sacrifice your honour in such a way."

Will frowned at his friend. What could Sam be thinking about as he entertained his former mistress in the theatre for all to see? His sisters could easily make mention of the situation to his betrothed. The Sam Bennet he had always known would never tarnish his honour in such a way or wound a lady. Many gentlemen had liaisons with courtesans even while married. Will had never thought Sam would be one of those men. In recent days, it felt as though he barely knew his friend. How had Sam kept all of this from him?

Will furrowed his brow. He had been distracted lately with concerns about his father and taking more control of Pemberley. He had less time for their usual frivolity and Sam had been forced to find other companionship.

"You are correct," Sam said and sighed.

"You do care for her," Will reminded him.

For most of their friendship, Sam had seemed enamoured with his neighbour. His letter to Will upon Miss Lucas accepting his hand in matrimony contained more effusions than Will had thought possible for one man to write. Last summer, he met Lucinda Johnson, and suddenly everything changed.

"But I love Lucy," Sam sighed.

"Do you?"

Sam rounded on his friend. "You question my affections? What do you know of love and romance?"

"I do not claim to know anything," Will conceded. "However, you have known Miss Lucas your entire life. You did not rush into any arrangement with her."

"It is a different thing entirely."

"How so?"

"Lucy is carrying my child. I can never just be done with her."

"A child?" Will's voice carried louder than he had intended.

Sam's eyes widened, but he looked over Will's shoulder. "Lizzy?"

"Papa wants you," Elizabeth said and turned away quickly.

"Blast," Sam shook his head.

"What will you tell her?"

"Nothing," Sam answered. "She is too young to know of these things."

Will frowned. He would not do the same to Georgiana. "She is not as young as you would think."

Sam assessed his friend. "You say this from your own thoughts about her?"

"She is more mature than I had envisioned, but she has also received attention from many of our Society."

Sam dropped his new carefree facade and straightened to his full height. He looked Will square in the eye when few others could. "You disappeared with her for quite some time yesterday. Can I trust you with my sister?"

Will's jaw tightened, and he measured his words. He had intended to speak with Sam about Harcourt's attention to Elizabeth and inquire why Will was so friendly with the man. Additionally, many others did take note of Elizabeth. The women and their matchmaking male relatives disliked her, but there was an appreciation in their gaze. Men across the lobby outright stared in approval. Sam may not have noticed, and Will may have been hesitant to admit it, but Elizabeth was full grown. However, this was not the time for such a conversation.

"Can I trust you with my sister?"

From the tone of Sam's voice and his earnest gaze, Will assumed his long-time friend mistook the meaning of his silence. Affronted, Will returned the look and tone. "Of course."

As of this moment, Elizabeth was far safer with him than her brother. Even if Will could not forget the sparkle in her eyes, the feel of her hand on his arm, and wonder about the taste of her ruby lips.

"Do not forget it, then," Sam said and pushed past Will to greet his father.

Will stood in silence for a moment. Years ago, he had lost a similarly gregarious friend. George Wickham had started displaying violent traits at Eton to fit in with the other boys. Sam seemed set for a similar path. While his situation of gambling with Harcourt might be understandable in light of his impending fatherhood, Will believed Sam had begun a doomed course. Had Sam confided in his father? What would Will's father do for a friend in such a scenario?

Pledged

Laughter from the theatre pulled Will's mind to the present. Reluctantly, he returned to the box. Elizabeth turned her head upon hearing his entry and beamed. Feeling as though someone had punched him in the gut, Will attempted to breathe normally and shift his eyes from hers. She was such an unexpected mix of everything he had never known he wanted in life. Beside her, Sam whispered something in her ear. She immediately returned her attention to the stage, but Sam glared at Will. Pursuing Elizabeth would strain his friendship with Sam and countless others. He could hardly suppose his father would support the match. His noble relations, while they greeted the Bennets, always mentioned their high hopes for him. Lady Catherine would likely wage war on all of Meryton. Marrying anyone but her daughter would be an insult. Marrying someone outside of the first tier of Society would send her prophesying doom for Pemberley and predicting his mother's ardent disapproval had she lived.

Taking his seat, Will kept his eyes on the stage but hardly knew what passed upon it. The carriage ride home was no more comfortable as his father chatted happily and Will moodily remained silent as he considered Sam's actions. Once home, the ladies went above stairs, and while the other men returned to the study for a nightcap, Will excused himself. Intending first to check on Georgiana, then to go to bed himself, he climbed the stairs to the appropriate floor and found Miss Graves weeping.

"Miss Graves, whatever is the matter?" he cried.

"Oh!" She turned her face from him but not before he saw a bruise forming on her cheek.

"Dear God! What has happened? Who struck you?"

"It is no matter. Forgive me for disturbing you." She hastily stood but winced.

Will came to her side and offered his arm for her to lean on. "You have not disturbed me. Pray, allow me to call for the housekeeper or send for the physician. You are not well and should not be out of bed."

"I ask that you do not fuss over me."

"My father would—"

"Whatever you do please do not tell him anything."

"Madam, I could not count myself as a gentleman if I left a lady in your state."

"I am only the governess. A servant. Forgettable and usually invisible."

"You are a person and a Darcy employee. We do not allow mistreatment of our staff from ourselves let alone others. Tell me who has harmed you."

Shaking her head, Miss Graves barely managed a whisper. "The master would never believe my word over his..."

Every muscle in Will's body tensed. He immediately understood who she referenced. George Wickham was his father's favourite as was recently displayed before her.

"Fear not," Will promised. "I will handle the entire thing. Allow me to assist you to your chamber."

"You are too kind," Miss Graves muttered but accepted his help.

"How was my sister today?" Will asked, hoping to fixate her thoughts on something pleasant.

"Miss Georgiana was in high spirits today, sir. She never gives me any trouble and is my most favourite charge that I have ever had."

"Indeed? How many have you had?"

"Six. Each position has only lasted a few months. I had hoped this one would be a more suitable situation and came highly recommended to me from my last mistress."

"I cannot imagine why a competent woman such as yourself is replaced so often."

Miss Graves blushed. "It is not for me to say, sir."

Will nearly missed a step on the stairs to understand she had been importuned so much. Were all men of his class so vile? "Do you wish for another position?"

"I do enjoy Miss Georgiana and have found Darcy House very comfortable until recently. If there were any way at all to remove certain recent additions to the household, then I would be most pleased to stay."

"The gentlemen will be leaving for an extended holiday in a few days. During that time I hope to find a solution to your troubles. I trust the ladies have not been a source of anxiety."

"No, indeed!" Miss Graves hastened to say. "The Miss Bennets always ask for permission before visiting Miss Darcy, and I can see their genuine affection for the girl."

"The Miss Bennets visit my sister?"

"Yes, they have spent much of their mornings in the nursery. Miss Elizabeth, especially, is partial to Miss Darcy. I believe she misses her sisters."

"Yes, she has several near Georgiana's age."

They arrived at the nursery chamber, and Will stopped outside. "I wish you would allow me to assist you further."

"There is no need, but I am truly thankful," Miss Graves answered. "Please accept my thanks and unending admiration."

Will began to refuse her thanks when he thought he heard a noise on the steps. However, looking over his shoulder, he saw nothing. "Sleep well, madam and please alert my valet should you require anything during the night."

Bowing to her, he left for his chambers. Georgiana would already be asleep, and Miss Graves needed privacy to tend to her injuries. Despite the melancholy event, Will smiled as he considered Elizabeth's obvious affection for his sister. What higher quality could he look for? While she might not meet his father's preference for fortune or rank, he could not overlook her care for his most favourite child. Meditating on such a possibility, Will steadfastly pushed worries about Sam and George Wickham aside for the night.

Elizabeth waited until she no longer heard the sounds of Miss Graves and Will outside the nursery chamber before exiting. She had come to read to Georgiana after the theatre and the girl insisted on hearing all about the excursion. Of course, there were many things Elizabeth could not tell anyone let alone a child.

Now, Elizabeth trembled as emotion surged through her. Why was Will at Miss Graves door? Her heart beat furiously and blood rushed to her face. That woman at the theatre clearly meant something to Sam. Elizabeth had seen longing in her brother's eyes and she had never seen him gaze at Charlotte Lucas in that way. Did Will feel for Miss Graves whatever it was Sam felt for the mysterious woman? He had insisted they dance and seemed most protective of her. Shaking her head, Elizabeth scolded herself. Why did it even matter to her?

Once downstairs, she turned down the hall to her chamber and saw Sam teeter near his door.

"Lizzy!" he called out loudly.

"Shh!" Elizabeth scolded and came closer. "Others may be asleep."

"You are correct," Sam said but did not whisper. "I wish I could rest as easy as some do." He fiddled with his door but had no success in opening it.

"You are still too loud," Elizabeth came closer to inspect his door as well.

"If you say so," he grinned.

At the closer proximity, Elizabeth caught a whiff of Sam's breath. "You are foxed!"

Sam shrugged. "Do not scold me, Lizzy. It is all I can do to live with myself."

Elizabeth's brow furrowed. She had no idea what he was going on about. "Let me help get you inside." She pushed him aside with her hip and turned the knob with ease.

Sam grinned when the door opened and took a step forward then staggered.

Elizabeth caught his arm. "Here, lean on me."

"Such a good sister," Sam smiled.

"Such an odd and odorous brother," Elizabeth laughed as they reached Sam's bed and he collapsed on it. She pulled off his boots.

"One day, when I find the best man in the world to make you a husband, he will be blessed to have you."

Unbidden, the image of Will came to her mind. Elizabeth blushed and shook her head. "No, I do not think any man will have me. Perhaps I will live with you and Charlotte forever."

Sam grimaced. "Why do you say that? I surely know there are cads and rakes in the world but there are good men too. Although, I am not sure there is one I would trust with you or my other sisters."

Elizabeth put her hands on her hips as she peered at her brother. "You know Mama says I am not ladylike enough. I know I will always have a home with you for you are the best brother."

Again, Sam's face contorted in a mixture of pain and regret. "Will you hate me, Lizzy, if I say I am not?"

Elizabeth laughed. "I will not hate you, but I will laugh at you. Sleep off your drink, brother. You make far more sense when sober."

"Come here," Sam held out his hand.

Elizabeth came closer and took it. "Do you need something? Water would be best."

"You are so good and pure," Sam said earnestly. "Have you enjoyed staying at Darcy House?"

"Yes," Elizabeth smiled and nodded.

"That is well but do not let this society alter you. The Lizzy Bennet I know is as carefree as a summer day. She has a refreshing, genuine laugh and carries herself with confidence."

"Sam," Elizabeth blushed, and words stuck in her throat.

"I would hate for you to be like Bingley's sisters."

"I promise, I will never be like them!"

"Good," Sam nodded then groaned. "And will you always think of me as you do now?"

Elizabeth squeezed her brother's hand. "You do not know how I have missed you each term when you leave for school. Must you stay for the entire summer with the Darcys?"

"I...I will be away for quite some time," he answered slowly. "You will forget all about me while staying with the Gardiners. Let me look at you now."

Elizabeth muffled a giggle as her brother cocked his head and squinted at her. With mussed hair and dishevelled clothes, he looked quite the hilarious picture and nothing like his usual charming and well-groomed self.

"Why, you are all grown up!" Sam said in astonishment. "When did you change from the little imp that was my sister?"

"I will always be your imp," Elizabeth said as tears filled her eyes. When their mother had died, Sam spent hours occupying her with various activities. She had followed him everywhere. Never once had he asked her to leave or seemed to regret her presence.

Elizabeth opened her mouth to say more but heard a snore come from her brother. He had fallen asleep even while sitting. Chuckling to herself, Elizabeth gently pushed his shoulders to the bed. Once there, Sam turned and brought his legs onto the mattress. Finding a coverlet in a chest, Elizabeth covered her brother and snuffed the candles. Before closing the door, she looked over her shoulder at him. No matter what happened with him and Charlotte, or with anybody else, he was her brother and she would always love him.

The following morning, Will arose and met his father in his study. For as long as Will could remember, George Darcy began work before breaking his fast. He dedicated two or three hours to business before greeting friends or family. Although in his early fifties, he had the energy of men half his age.

Will knocked on the door and was bade to enter. His father did not look up. "Father, may I speak with you on a most disturbing subject?"

Mr. Darcy returned his pen to the ink pot and folded his hands on his desk, giving his son all of his attention. "There must be some urgency behind this topic."

"Indeed, there is. Last night, I found Miss Graves sobbing on the stairs outside the nursery. A bruise was forming on her cheek, and I believe she had been accosted and assaulted by George."

The older man clenched his jaw and gave his son a sharp look. "Do you have proof of this? Did she accuse him?"

"No. She did not want me meddling and did not wish to name her attacker."

"Then perhaps you had better listen to her."

"Sir! How can you say that when you have a daughter? At this very moment, you have a house full of ladies that might be his next target."

"Yesterday was Miss Graves day off. She was out of the house most of the day. Anyone might have harmed her. I do not believe anyone in this household capable of such a thing." Mr. Darcy rubbed his temples. "If it eases your mind, I will speak to Miss Graves about sending a footman to accompany her when she is out. The new one, Annesley, might do."

Mr. Darcy motioned for his son to sit. Sighing, he said, "You have no proof Wickham was behind the incident. Think about it, son. Do you think a young man who has been raised nearly as a brother to yourself, who comes from such good stock and reared with all the bounty Pemberley can offer is capable of such a thing? What would make him strike Miss Graves tonight when he has never done such a thing before?" Mr. Darcy turned red and pounded his fists on his desk. "I have tolerated your dislike of him long enough."

"You are mistaken, sir, if you believe there have been no similar incidents. Why else have you had so many governesses for Georgiana?"

Will's father scoffed. "Mrs. Reynolds always claimed they had found another position they enjoyed better. More pay, time in London, holidays with their families. Not everyone is suited to our lifestyle. Additionally, they all left months after George had last been in their company and I never saw a sign of injury upon them."

"I think it likely that Miss Graves is the first to refuse his attempts at seduction."

"Come, Will, that is beneath you. George is a handsome lad with charm and money enough that he would not need to resort to seducing my staff for his sport. Besides, he has too much honour. Every gentleman knows never to touch a servant." He picked up his quill and returned his attention to his letter once more. "Just as they know a friend's sister is off limits. Therefore I have no reason to worry about either you or George."

Will took a step back, feeling as though he had been punched in the gut. His father knew of his attraction to Elizabeth? Evidently, he also disapproved and hoped to remind him of the code of honour among gentlemen. Taking a deep breath, Will scrutinised his father's face once more. No, the older gentleman did not know of Will's admiration for Elizabeth. He merely spoke of something on which he believed Will could understand.

"Now, if you do not have proof or anything else to say, leave me to my work. This holiday is planned for you and your friends—even old ones you no longer find pleasing—and I must finish before we can leave."

"Yes, sir," Will said and bowed.

Throughout the morning, he went through the motions. He read for a short while in the library until he heard others on the steps and joined them for breakfast. Elizabeth refused to meet his eyes and Sam seemed less jovial than usual. By the time the Bingleys and Richard arrived, the young people had adjourned to the drawing room and a headache burned behind Will's eyes.

"How terribly droll this morning is," Caroline observed. "Louisa and I were just saying how bored we are."

"Oh, yes," Louisa agreed and nodded. "We were."

Will internally rolled his eyes. How was it the elder sister did nothing but parrot the younger?

"A game of billiards would be enjoyable," Bingley suggested.

Caroline threw a hand to her throat. "Billiards? Oh, we ladies could not possibly play!"

Out of the corner of his eye, Will saw Elizabeth smirk.

"I am sure we could all do nearly anything gentlemen do, although not with the same degree of accomplishment. However, the same is true even amongst our own sex."

Caroline narrowed her eyes. "Yes, you are correct, Eliza. Some ladies are far more accomplished than others."

Not this again. "I propose a game of Sardines."

Each head swung in Will's direction.

"You want to play Sardines," Richard slowly said.

Will was unsure why he suggested it except it would require the others to be quiet and if he were lucky, he could be the first to hide and therefore have solitude. He hated the powerless feeling he had as he had attempted to help Miss Graves. Additionally, Sam seemed to be in no mood to cheer him up, and Elizabeth seemed to have taken a sudden dislike of him. He needed privacy to sort out his thoughts. "I will hide first."

"Now, wait a moment," Bingley said. "You will know all the best places to hide. "That is not fair."

Sam nodded. "All of us men will know. Let one of the ladies go first."

"I should like to try," Elizabeth said with a twinkle in her eyes.

"You would," Caroline muttered not nearly quiet enough.

Elizabeth continued as though she had not heard. "I am exceptionally good at hiding. It is one of my many accomplishments."

Caroline glared at Elizabeth, but the others agreed to let her hide first. While Elizabeth wandered off, Will wondered how he could manage to look without being caught with the Miss Bingleys following his every move. "I think we should say every person is to search without help."

"That is not the traditional way to play," Richard observed.

"We are no longer children," Will shrugged.

"Some of us are," Caroline chirped.

"Would you rather visit Georgiana in the Nursery?" Will asked.

Caroline's grin vanished, and she paled.

Sam held out his watch. The others made small talk while they waited for the time to search for Elizabeth. Will considered unfairly breaking the rules. Yes, he did know the hiding areas in the house. Rather than search for Elizabeth, he would hide.

At the appointed time, the group dispersed and went in different directions. Will entered the library and shut the door behind himself. He walked directly to the wall between the library and his father's dressing room. The secret cupboard would be just deep enough for one or two people...or had been when he was a child. Now, it would be considerably cramped, but he would bear it to have a few minutes away from Caroline and Louisa Bingley.

He opened it up and heard a feminine gasp. At the same time, there was a sound near the library door. Small hands gripped him by the lapel and pulled him inside the cupboard. The door clicked shut just as the other opened. As Will's eyes adjusted to the dark, he could see Elizabeth's shocked face. Not that he needed to see her to know it was her. One, she was supposed to be hiding. Two, her scent filled the place. Her lavender fragrance relaxed him and soothed his aching head.

"What are you doing here?" she whispered.

"Hiding," he answered.

"Hiding?"

"I did not expect you to locate this place. It is hardly large enough for the game." Each additional person who found Elizabeth would need to enter the cupboard. As it was, their backs were pressed against the walls, and only the merest distance stood between their bodies. Elizabeth must have been as uncomfortable as Will because she could not stop fidgeting.

"I did not expect to be found. However, you were supposed to be searching. Confess it. You were cheating at the game to avoid the others."

Will arched a brow as perspiration began to roll down his back. The little cupboard trapped the summer heat and the heat of their bodies only added to it. "It is my home. I may go where I choose."

"And slight your guests?"

Will avoided her question. "Why did you choose this place to hide? Why did you offer yourself as the first to play if you did not want to avoid the others?"

"You suggested the game first. You—"

"Quiet," Will hissed. He heard footsteps approach. Elizabeth fidgeted and knocked her elbow into him. "Be still!"

"I cannot help it," she sighed. "You are so large! So tall and so broad!" Elizabeth's breath quickened. "It is unbearably hot."

Unable to raise his hand to cover her mouth, Will silenced her the only way he could. He leaned down and placed his lips on hers.

Instantly, arousal shot through his body. He had never known the primal urge now coursing through him. Elizabeth melted against him, her mouth meeting his even as he began to demand hot kisses. Pressing his tongue against her lips, he slid into the cavern of her mouth. His eyes rolled in the back of his head at the sweet taste of her. Chocolate from her breakfast. It was good he could not move, he could not take her in his arms. He could not press her against the wall and have his hand run over her flesh or lift up her skirt.

Will's lips left hers, desperate for the taste of her skin. Elizabeth moaned, bringing some of his mind back to the present. Still, he trailed down her neck, pressing kisses on the sensitive flesh until he found her pulse point and could feel her heart's rapid beats for him. Elizabeth shuddered against him, and he dropped his head to her shoulder.

"Elizabeth," Will rasped as both of their chests rose and fell in quick spurts. "Everything about you endangers my sanity. One look from you and I am undone."

Elizabeth stiffened. "Get out."

Will brought his head up and tried to meet her eyes but she turned her head. He could see the scarlet red of one flushed cheek.

"Forgive me," he whispered. "A terrible lapse of judgement...I should never have..."

"Get out," she said, but her voice wavered.

Dear God, he had made her cry. His first real kiss with a woman reduced her to tears. Peeking out the cupboard door, he exited without a backward glance.

Chapter Five

After Will left, Elizabeth remained in the cupboard alone for nearly an hour. Grateful for the solitude, Elizabeth attempted to push aside her intense attraction to Will in light of what she had seen last night.

Elizabeth had visited the nursery to say goodnight to Georgiana but found her asleep. The girl reminded Elizabeth of her younger siblings so very much, and she had not anticipated missing them. However, it was her first time away from home but not with relatives. She had soon learned that while her sisters could be bothersome, there was great comfort in their familiarity.

After Georgiana fell asleep, Elizabeth neared the nursery door when she heard the voices of Will and Miss Graves. She could not make out their words. Inching open the door, she saw Miss Graves crying and Will leading her to her chamber. Elizabeth knew enough that no gentleman should be near a lady's door. At the theatre, it was clear Sam, and possibly Will too, had some private liaison with a raven-haired beauty. Later that evening, Elizabeth saw Will with his sister's governess. She had attempted to tell herself it made no difference, despite her growing infatuation with the man. Then, he kissed her, and it seemed the whole world resided in the space where their lips met.

While they had not started their friendship on the best foot, Elizabeth had thought Will began to have a tendre for her. He declared as much. Now, it seemed he did nothing more than play with her while he paid his attentions on other women. Although sheltered in the ways of men, Elizabeth understood there were some ladies considered unmarriageable. She knew men often spent time with the ladies and received physical pleasure from them. The woman at the theatre indeed seemed like one, and the heir of Pemberley could never marry his sister's governess.

Elizabeth's heart sank as she reconsidered Will's words from the theatre. She, too, was considered insufficient. Rather than avoid her, Will sought her out. Star-crossed lovers would be terrible enough, but the way he kissed her in the cupboard without a word regarding courtship must mean he had no respect for her.

Heat slapped Elizabeth's cheeks, and blood rushed through her veins as her heart pounded. How foolish she had been! Why did she ever change her opinion of the young man? She had been charmed by his appearance and their common interests. Although she could find no fault with his behaviour as a brother, had she not witnessed proof of his father's displeasure? Of Mr. Darcy, she had no reason to doubt. After all, her father trusted the man. As for general civility, Will immediately lacked the hospitality a host should offer his guests. If she needed further proof, she needed to look no further than he had earned the admiration of the Miss Bingleys.

For a moment, Elizabeth's eyes welled with tears and shame threatened to strangle her heart. What a blow to her pride! She had not thought she would be so susceptible to such empty considerations with a suitor. His handsomeness and wealth had blinded her to the fact that he lacked the morality and character she needed for a husband.

"Husband!"

When had she turned into a ninny that believed every gentleman she met was a prospective husband? When had she turned her thoughts to matrimony? She was only sixteen. However, one day, she would have to walk down the church's aisle and face a man at the altar. She would vow to honour and obey. To herself, Elizabeth promised it would only be to a man she loved. Still, while she could not say all her examples of matrimony were ideal, in general, she had more examples of married ladies than spinsters, and of the two categories, the spinsters had always seemed the least happy and most pitiable.

Elizabeth's step-mother had insisted on putting her out at sixteen. She had declared Elizabeth would need the additional years to find a suitor due to her headstrong and bookworm ways. Suddenly, it felt as though a noose were tightening around Elizabeth's neck. Her breath came fast, but still it seemed there was not enough air in her lungs. She had to escape this cupboard. She needed space!

No longer caring for the game and if anyone discovered her, she fled her hiding spot. There was a narrow staircase next to Mr. Darcy's study, and Elizabeth raced up it until she nearly collided with Miss Graves.

"Miss Elizabeth!" the older lady caught Elizabeth by the elbows lest she fall down the stairs. "Good heavens!"

"Forgive me," Elizabeth panted and moved to push past the governess.

"Pray, forgive the intrusion, but you seem unwell. You have been so kind to me, allow me to assist you."

"It is nothing," Elizabeth dissembled.

"What could make you run with such abandon and a wild look in your eye? Please, you may tell me. You are not alone in your troubles."

"What do you mean?" Elizabeth asked. Did she care to hear how this woman also loved Will Darcy? At the weight of her thoughts, Elizabeth flushed then paled. Her legs buckled.

Miss Graves caught Elizabeth and brought her down to sit on the stairs. "I must insist now! Mr. Darcy would never forgive himself if he injured you as well."

Elizabeth's brow furrowed and for the first time, she noticed the bruise on Miss Graves' cheek. Curls which usually framed her face were pushed behind her ear. "I am uninjured, but it appears you are not. Did he..." Tears streamed down Elizabeth's face to consider the possibility that Will could abuse anyone. "Did he assault you? Did he force you?"

Miss Graves shook her head but would not speak.

"Please, I must know," Elizabeth said as she laid a calming hand on the woman's arm. "You had said I was not alone and offered assistance. Why do you not allow me to extend the same courtesy to you?"

A sob wrenched from Miss Graves' mouth as a shudder wracked her body. "I will confide in you," she muttered with a shaky breath.

Elizabeth wrapped her arms around the lady and rubbed her back soothingly, the same as she would for one of her sisters. After several minutes, Miss Graves gathered herself enough to speak.

"He did not force me, but he did not take no for an answer. He thought I would submit if injured. I do not know what might have happened to me if he had not heard the noise of an occupant in the nursery."

Elizabeth flushed as she considered she must have been the cause for the interruption. "You must tell Mr. Darcy. Come, let us go to him at once."

Miss Graves held back. "No, in my experience it is best to keep my head down. Master Will informs me that the men are to leave in a few days. He promised nothing, but he hopes to keep Wickham," she spat the name, "from returning to the house."

Elizabeth started at the information. Mr. Wickham assaulted the lady? What about Will outside of the governess' chamber last night?

"I must only bear with the fear for a few more days. I have never been more afraid in my life but also never more hopeful. You must understand, I have had to leave several positions due to the unseemly desires of men. They have never been violent before, but there was always the fear of a reoccurrence at the next situation."

Miss Graves raised her shoulders and strength infused her frame. "I will soon be free of this concern, and I will fight to keep this position. I love Miss Darcy too much and have the greatest esteem for Mr. Darcy."

"And Master Fitzwilliam?" The words escaped Elizabeth before she could help it.

"The young master?" Miss Graves voice rose in pitch as her brow furrowed. "Well, I barely have said more than a few words to him. I do thank him for assisting me last night. He says he will help me, but I do not want to cause trouble between him and his father."

"You told him what happened?"

Miss Graves nodded. "I was overwrought. When I came to my senses, I begged him to say nothing, but I do not know that he will."

"Will Darcy will do whatever he pleases and deems best regardless of the desires of others," Elizabeth observed wryly.

"I cannot condemn the gentleman for having a superior sense of honour and duty."

Elizabeth slowly nodded. The woman had correctly summarized Will. His obstinacy could be annoying but came from the best of intentions. How unfairly she had accused and condemned him!

"Forgive me," Miss Graves said. "I fear I have made this entirely about me and it was you who needed assistance."

"Do not apologise. I am entirely well, now. I only needed physical exertion and wanted to be away from all the finery of the public rooms."

"You come from the country, do you not?"

Elizabeth nodded. "I live near a market town in Hertfordshire. I am used to long daily walks in solitude. I fear I do not thrive in proper drawing rooms and under the scrutiny of the most fashionable or rich."

"You are young yet," Miss Graves smiled at her. "You may find as you age that more of London and the fine life appeals to you."

The sound of the door at the top of the stairs opening reminded Elizabeth of their location. They cordially parted but as she returned to her chamber, Miss Graves' words of fear mixed with hope resounded in her ears. Such conflicting emotions could create great anxiety, and Elizabeth's heart pounded in her ears as she acknowledged it must be the cause for her mental abuse of Will. She loved him. It both terrified and excited her.

After Will had left Elizabeth's hiding place, he set out to find Wickham. The others would be disappointed he did not play the game with them, but it had never been his intention to do so. If his father would not see reason regarding his favourite, then perhaps Will could convince Wickham to leave Darcy House.

Will found him in the kitchen, trying to charm the cook into a sample of the evening's meal. "George, I would speak with you."

Will noticed the nearly imperceptible change in his long-ago friend's countenance. Pure hatred emitted from his eyes. Will wondered what he had ever done to deserve such malice from the man he had once loved as a brother. The others saw no change in his demeanour, however, and Wickham kept up his usual charm.

"Certainly."

Will noted that Wickham avoided the issue of having to address him by name. As they were no longer boys or even friends, calling him by an informal name would be inappropriate given the difference in their stations. However, Wickham could never bear to say "sir" or "Master Fitzwilliam" as the servants, and his father, did. Will could almost pity Wickham for the awkward situation. Mr. Darcy had thought he had done a kindness to his steward's son by raising him with his heir, but all it did was raise Wickham's expectations and taste for the fine things in life.

Wickham approached. Once out of the hearing of others, he raised his brows and spoke in a derisive tone. "Well?"

Will came in close to the other man. Towering over him by several inches, Wickham had to tilt his head back to meet his eyes. "I know what you have done," Will said through clenched teeth. "You will not get away with it this time."

"What is it that you think I have done? Do you have any proof?"

"You have assaulted Miss Graves. You have, at last, met a lady who will not succumb to your charm and abandon her reputation."

"Oh, I see. You suppose I have harmed her," Wickham smirked. "I am sorry to hear she has been injured. She is a pretty lass. However, did she name me? Were there witnesses?"

"Those are charming words and I daresay would better suit a man intended for court than the cloth."

Wickham stroked his jaw. "It would certainly be more profitable, but I would hate to disappoint your dear father. I notice you did not answer my questions."

Sick of Wickham's games, Will grabbed him by the lapel, rejoicing when Wickham flinched. "Leave this house. I will provide a handsome sum for you to find your amusements this summer elsewhere. When I return from holiday, I will contact you with arrangements so you never need step foot in a Darcy residence again."

Wickham pulled back and smoothed out his coat, seemingly unaffected by Will's display. "I see you are feeling powerful and with deep pockets. Coming of age has given you freedom of money, it appears. However, we both know your father will not support you in any attempt of ousting me while he lives."

Incensed, Will glowered. "Mind your words, George. One day I will be master of Pemberley, and I will have no charity for you."

"What a sad day, indeed, that will be. I notice you seem to rejoice at the idea of your father's demise. I would expect nothing less from an arrogant and pampered but disloyal cur such as you."

"How dare you put words in my mouth? How dare you—"

"No! How dare you! Perhaps you might need to force ladies, but I have never needed to resort to such." Wickham raised a brow. "On second thought, they would easily open their legs for your pocketbook. Instead of chastising me, perhaps you ought to consider your friend residing here. I have heard rumours of Young Bennet running with a rough crowd in recent months."

Momentarily silenced by the shred of truth in Wickham's words, Will had no ready retort. A servant rounded the corner and hovered behind Wickham.

"Pardon me. The master desires Mr. Wickham for a game of billiards," the servant said.

"Very good," Wickham said and nodded at the servant. Without another word, he left Will in the hall.

Controlling the impulse to stalk after them and pull Wickham into his father's study by the collar, Will clenched and unclenched his fists.

When his breathing had returned to normal, he returned to the drawing room intending to ask the gentlemen to join him for a ride in the park. Upon his arrival, he was told Elizabeth felt ill and had taken to her chamber. Was she avoiding him?

Convinced that Elizabeth was upset after their encounter, Will bided his time until the others left to dress for dinner. What could he say to her? Never in his life had he given into his base impulses before. He had never hinted at his growing attraction to her. She was only sixteen and had limited interactions with gentlemen. Most likely, Will had terrified her. He never said anything of courtship or marriage, and she must presume that he had no honourable intentions. The thought that he could in any way be similar to George Wickham disgusted him.

As Will dressed for the evening, he considered his choices for the future. While Mr. Darcy did not support his son marrying his cousin, the older gentleman did have expectations for Will's eventual bride. The average age most gentlemen married was close to thirty. However, Will did not have that luxury. He was the only son of an old family and a large estate. He was expected to marry young and begin producing the next generation of Darcys to look after Pemberley. While there was no entail on the estate and therefore Georgiana could always inherit. However, Will knew his father hoped for his son to inherit and sire another line for succession. Although Mr. Darcy was friends with Mr. Bennet, Will doubted he would approve of Elizabeth as a match for his son.

Duty and expectation were not unknown to Will. He had always endeavoured to live up to his father's expectations. Most would call him an ever-dutiful son. In recent months, however, Will's relationship with his father had become strained due to George Wickham. It was evident to Will that his father did not trust him regarding Wickham. The fact that his employees might be injured or harmed by him frustrated Will to the core. For many years now, he had seen vicious propensities in Wickham. At school, Will had been entirely powerless to protect other boys from Wickham's schemes or taunts. As for ladies, they had always seem to be willing bed-partners. When the time came for their eventual disenchantment with the cad, typically with a child on the way, Will instructed the housekeeper to provide for them. As far as Will knew, Miss Graves was the only one who refused Wickham what he wanted. In recent years, Will had come to his father several times about Wickham. As Will never had verifiable proof, the other man always seemed to wiggle out of any accusation.

His father now had it in his head that Will's arguments were based on jealousy alone. Will admitted to himself there was some truth to his father's assertions. As a child, he had been jealous of his father's attention to the steward's son. Sighing, Will realised he would not be able to convince his father without Miss Graves' confession.

Also on Will's mind was Wickham's charge against Sam. While Will struggled with the new dynamics of his relationship with his father, Sam had been growing increasingly distant and finding new friends of a different crowd. Sam's association with Lord Harcourt proved to Will that his friend was in over his head. As much as Will was powerless against Wickham, so he was against Sam's choices. The most he could do was attempt to explain to Sam the dangerous path he was now on.

Although Sam would not welcome Will's desire for courtship with his sister, it would perhaps put them on some level ground. Will could not condone the notion of Sam breaking his engagement to his betrothed. However, Will, at last, understood the pull of one's heart. He had been defenceless against his own heart. He had been taught to resist the seduction of ladies who desired his money and name. Elizabeth seemed entirely unaffected by both. If she esteemed and respected him, it was for his character and because they had become friends. The fire that sparked between them rested squarely on Will's shoulders. While Elizabeth had not pulled back, she had not instigated their intimacy. Now that he had a chance of passion and happiness his grasp, he could not let it go. Sam would fight Will on desiring his sister; however, in the end, Will hoped Sam could understand why he must follow his heart. To that end, Will knew he needed to support Sam in following his.

Determined to seek out his friend and let him know his growing attachment to Elizabeth, Will felt in control of the situation again. Leaving his chamber, he hoped he would see Elizabeth before dinner. As he walked down the guest wing, he saw her light figure.

"Elizabeth," Will whispered.

Elizabeth paused and turned to see who called her name. Will reached for her hand and pulled her around the corner so they might have privacy. "Have you been avoiding me?"

"Do you think I have a reason to avoid you?"

"I wanted to apologize for my behaviour," Will said. "I believe I scared you."

"What was it that you believe frightened me?"

"If you do not wish to speak on it further, I will abide by your wishes. However, I wish you to know that I have come to feel very strongly for you."

"As your friend's sister?"

Will shook his head. "You mean more, so much more to me than that." Will searched Elizabeth's eyes. "I told you already that I lose my wits around you. The truth is I never want that to stop. You enrapture me. With you, I see the world in ways I have never seen it before. You bring a lightness to my heart."

A flush had crept up Elizabeth's face during Wills impassioned speech. He could not resist the urge to stroke her cheek and touch her soft flesh. "I am falling in love with you, Elizabeth Bennet. And I ought to have considered that you deserved better for your first kiss. "

Elizabeth's blush deepened, making Will grin as his supposition seemed correct. He had been the first man to ever kiss her. He vowed to himself, he would be her last.

Despite her embarrassment, Elizabeth met Will's eyes and smiled. "How would you kiss me then?"

Will grinned. He came in closer to Elizabeth. Her back was to the wall and he placed one hand to the side of her head and leaned against the wall. His other hand still held her cheek. Will's chest rapidly rose and fell, and her eyelashes fluttered in anticipation.

"Like this!" He muttered as his head moved toward hers.

Softly, Will kissed her cheek and turned her head and kissed the other. He kissed her eyelids and felt her lashes flutter beneath his lips. He kissed her forehead. He lowered his arm that had been against the wall and trailed it down her arm, until it circled her waist. Pulling Elizabeth closer, he peered down at her. The image of her waiting, ready, desiring his kiss would remain imprinted in his mind forever. When Will judged her impatient enough, he softly placed his lips over hers. The quiet sigh and feel of her smile against him in response, answered every question he had.

Elizabeth pressed her lips against Will's in return. Together, they explored each other's mouths for many minutes until, with a groan, Will trailed kisses down Elizabeth's neck. Elizabeth's head rolled backward, giving him greater access. Again, he could feel her rapid pulse and hear her breaths. What began as sweet exploration turned passionate. He now wrapped both arms around Elizabeth as she clung to his neck. Their bodies lined up between them. His hands rubbed up and down her back, measuring her trim waist and lingering on her hips. Elizabeth gasped, and Will stifled it with a deep kiss, his tongue sweeping into her hot mouth.

He was losing control in a hallway near her bedroom. An instinct he would rather not admit he had reminded him of all the beds nearby. The greater and more honourable part of Will recalled she was his best friend's sister. A step sounded on the hallway and Will sprang apart from Elizabeth.

"Will!"

Will turned to see the angry visage of his friend.

Chapter Six

Sam stormed off and Will gulped, following his friend to his chamber.

"You have precisely one minute to explain to me why I should not pummel you for touching my sister, let alone in such a way."

"You do not understand." Will held his hands up to calm his friend. "It is not what it appears."

"It looks like you were in the middle of seducing my sister right under my nose. I trusted you!"

"I love her!" Will's eyes widened as he realized what he had confessed. None of this was going according to his plan. He was supposed to ask Sam and Mr. Bennet for permission to court Elizabeth. Then he would ask for her hand. During his summer away, he would have time to consider his method of courtship. They were still so young and his father would probably not approve the match. Will had no reason to think they could marry quickly. He would have to tell her as much. A gem like Elizabeth would not wait forever. However, Will did have some independence now and if push came to shove, they could marry. He hoped for both their sakes that their families would approve and not keep them waiting for too long.

"I am still waiting, Will. You say you love her. What you know of love?"

"I know I have not supported you as you would like, given your situation and feelings for Lucy. However, now I understand. The heart wants what it wants, and no amount of logic can gainsay it."

"Are you saying it is illogical to be in love with my sister?"

"I am saying nothing of the sort. I am not unaware of the arguments you or anyone else have against the match. I told them to myself and, if you will recall, before we even met I was not predisposed to like her."

"Oh yes, the Darcy pride. How could I forget that?" Sam said derisively.

"What does my pride have to do with this?"

"It has every with this! Did you think I did not approve of your admiration for my sister because I found your character wanting?"

"There is a code amongst gentlemen that we will not touch a friend's sister."

"I would be more worried about that if you had ever touched anybody," Sam laughed.

"So, you worry about Charles attentions toward Jane?" Will could not understand Sam's position on the subject.

"The Darcys and Bingleys are two entirely different worlds. I do not worry for Charles because it is Charles. He might like Jane now, but next week he will move on. We are spending many months away, and Jane has a new suitor every week. She is too accustomed to men to let her heart grow attached so quickly." Sam sighed and slumped in a chair, waving for Will to do likewise.

"And you believe that Elizabeth and I would feel too deeply?"

"I know that you would not leap into anything without thoroughly thinking it through."

Will disagreed but kept it to himself. He did not have the self-control his friends seemed to think he did. "I imagine it is much like when you first met Lucy."

"I thought only of my arousal when I met Lucy." Sam glared at Will. "Would you like to try again and explain how this is not the same and how you can love Elizabeth so much within a matter of days?"

Will sighed and rested his elbows on his knees. "I have recounted it to myself enough in the past day or so as I wondered how I got here so unaware. I can only think that I was in the middle before I knew I even began. Elizabeth is beautiful and I am attracted to her. However, there are one hundred other things that appeal to me and have greater weight. Every day I discover something new. I am infinitely fascinated by her." Will shrugged. "For once, I do not feel like the heir of Pemberley. Elizabeth wants nothing from me. I am free to be myself with her and she makes me want to be better in ways I never thought of before."

"That is all well and good, but you do not know what you are asking of her," Sam placed a hand on Will shoulder. "She is only sixteen and is unprepared for your world. Your father will not approve. Both of your aunts have their sights set on others for you. The very people Lizzy would need for support in your world would never approve of her.

"What are you saying?" Will asked, madness threatening to rise within him.

"Forget about my sister. You have two very different destinies."

Will staring at his friend in slack-jawed disbelief. He would fight for Elizabeth. He would not give her up. However, as he observed his friend, Sam's shoulders slumped in dejection. Perhaps his words were far more about his own situation than about Will's. "I cannot agree with your opinion on these matters. However, I did want to speak to you on other subjects. Lord Harcourt seems to have Elizabeth in his sights."

"Surely not," Sam laughed. "I assure you, he prefers worldlier ladies."

"At the very least, his mode of conversation with her is impertinent and makes her uncomfortable. I implore you, speak to him."

"If you wish, but I see nothing more than the jealous concern of a suitor. Do not forget I know about your possessive side. Do you still hate Wickham for gaining your father's attention and approval so easily?"

Will let out a frustrated sigh. "Why is it you trust Harcourt at all? Confess it; you have more than a passing acquaintance with the man that all of London knows is a devious rake and a gambler."

Sam opened and closed his mouth several times before any sound came out. He held his hands out and let out a dejected side. "I will tell you the truth. I needed money for Lucy's sake. I went around to banks and other creditors, but Harcourt was the only one that would have mercy on me."

"Dear God! Could you not have asked me?"

"I did not think you would approve. I was ashamed. Everything I have said about London Society eating up Elizabeth has happened to me…" Sam hung his head.

Will could not find it in his heart to criticise his friend. "How much do you owe? You should not be in debt to such a man."

Sam shook his head. "I cannot ask for you to pay. I would rather take my chances being in debt to him than take advantage of our friendship."

Will stared at his friend for a long time. "Is it very much?"

"It would not matter if it was a mere twenty pounds. I would not ask it of you."

"You spoke of the Darcy pride, but I perceive your pride at work here as well."

"I made a mess of things, but it is my burden to clean it up." Sam stood and walked to the door. "Now, it is time for us to join the others for dinner."

"I will be speaking to your father about Elizabeth soon."

"You had better talk to your father first." Sam shook his head. "Do not be in a hurry to seal your fate, Will. You may think you love her now, but only time will tell. Learn from my mistakes."

As they were no longer in the privacy of Sam's chambers, Will said no more on the subject and followed his friend downstairs. Sam said he would not accept money from him, but Will still intended to make a substantial withdrawal on the morrow. Some would go to Sam if he would take it, and the rest to Wickham so he would find a life away from the Darcy family.

Throughout the meal, he could not keep his eyes from falling upon Elizabeth. She looked lovely, but more than that, she looked as though she belonged at a Darcy table. She sat near his father. Now and then, she said something to make the older gentleman laugh. George Darcy had a different temperament than his children, and the death of his wife sobered him, but he still enjoyed amusement. It was why George Wickham became his favourite. Elizabeth's humour, however, was a different sort than Wickham's. She involved all others around her in conversation as well. Will gleaned that she remembered interests that she shared with the other guests and chose those topics to converse on. She had all the qualities an excellent hostess should have.

On previous nights, Will's father had not encouraged the ladies to separate from the gentlemen. This evening, he maintained tradition. As it happened, Lord and Lady Fitzwilliam dined with them. Will's aunt served as hostess and led the ladies to the drawing room. The first few minutes of the customary separation from the ladies passed in the ordinary way. Port and brandy were poured while cigars were smoked. Before too long, Mr. Darcy approached Will and asked for them to speak privately. Will agreed, although uncertain of what would follow.

The older gentleman shut the door to his study and motioned to a chair. Will sat and his father took the seat next to him rather than behind the imposing desk.

"Well, I had not thought that I had landed upon the truth so much when I mentioned that you would not enter a relationship with Sam's sister. It appears I was mistaken."

Will's mind raced. Had they been seen? "There's nothing to say on the matter because I have not asked anything of the lady. I am aware of Sam's disapproval and am attempting to overcome his arguments."

"But you cannot doubt her answer. A girl like Elizabeth Bennet would jump at a chance to marry you. Beware, my son, for you are now of age and finished with University. Many ladies will try to capture you in their claws."

Will shook his head. "I will not abide any criticism of her character. Miss Elizabeth is nothing of that sort. She could not care less about fortune or rank. She is not like the other young ladies I have encountered who simper and fawn. I sometimes think she has more strength of character than many a man I know, for she will not play Society's games. She will not bend her moral compass to suit the whims of others." As Will spoke, he clenched his fists. This man would malign his friend's daughter without knowing her. Meanwhile, he condoned Wickham and refused to criticize him. Even Sam had bent his honour to suit his needs.

"Pardon me," Mr. Darcy said with genuine remorse. "I did not mean to offend. You are correct. I do not know her well enough to make these assertions. Might I remind you that you also do not know her well?"

"I have done much more than merely dine with her in the last few days. She has awakened parts of my soul that I never knew existed. There can be no doubt about her loyalty. With her beauty and charm, she would have no shortage of wealthy suitors in any circle in which she walked. At the theatre, many gentlemen peered at her with an approving eye. Lord Harcourt did not make his admiration secret at all."

Mr. Darcy sighed. "Harcourt has always loved the ladies. His admiration of Miss Elizabeth does not mean an offer would be imminent."

"That is true," Will conceded. "But Miss Elizabeth is hardly aware of his true nature or his reputation. Many would hear his rank and see the quality of his fashionable attire and assume he would be a worthy suitor to try to entrap. I have seen dozens of ladies operate similarly, including the Miss Bingleys."

"Yes. Joseph's daughters are quite cunning."

"Indeed." Will sighed. "I respect you, Father. However, I will choose my own bride and in my own time. There are qualities I must consider for the sake of Pemberley's future that go beyond its purse strings. We are on the cusp of a new world and a new way of running things. Merely finding a noble daughter with a hefty dowry is not the only way to keep funds afloat."

Mr. Darcy raised his brows. "Do you mean to suggest I married your mother simply because she was a good match?"

"Whatever feelings came after the ceremony, I believe you have confessed enough for me to say with some assurance that it was an alliance and not a love match."

"Precisely!" Mr. Darcy nodded emphatically. "Those feelings did come after the ceremony, so why do you think they would not come for you?"

"I have never argued with you about this in the past. I appreciate that you have supported me against Lady Catherine and her desire for me to marry Anne. I know now I can never marry a woman without loving her, because my heart is already engaged."

"Be reasonable, Fitzwilliam. You have known her for less than a week."

Will rose to his feet. "And yet men that I have known for many years, perhaps even all my life, give me reason to question their loyalty and their character. Why do you persist in ignoring George Wickham's faults? Why are you on such friendly terms with Harcourt?

Will's father turned red. "I do not need to defend myself to you. I cannot tell you who to marry. You have some income from your mother, but even if it were in my power to completely cut you off, I would not. You have given me no reason to distrust you, but it hurts me to hear that you have no faith in my judgment. Perhaps when you are older, you shall see things differently." Mr. Darcy hung his head.

Will took a step toward his father. "Forgive me, Father. I look forward to the additional responsibilities I will receive in the autumn. Your trust means the world to me, but I will not compromise my beliefs for you."

Mr. Darcy stood and placed a hand on his son's shoulder. "No, I would not wish for you to do so. I cannot say that I approve of your choice and I caution you to not be in any rush. However, I have confidence in you. I will support any decision you make in this matter." Mr. Darcy's eyes flitted to the clock in the study. "Now, it is time to rejoin the ladies."

The two men returned to the dining room before Mr. Darcy announced his intention to go to the drawing room. The others followed him. Will looked around the chamber and noted both Miss Bennets absent.

"Sam, where are your sisters?" Will asked.

"I have been informed by your aunt that Lizzy claimed a headache and Jane went upstairs with her."

Sam's attention was drawn away, but Will believed the situation unusual. He scanned the room once more and noted Miss Caroline Bingley's pleased expression as she sat next to Lady Fitzwilliam. Will came closer to hear their conversation.

"You are so charming, Miss Caroline. I regret I was not able to speak with you more at the theatre."

"Perhaps we may be thankful after all that Miss Elizabeth became indisposed."

"Yes," Lady Fitzwilliam nodded. "She surely gave her opinions most decidedly, although she was charming enough during the meal."

"Some women can only be agreeable when there are men around to impress."

Louisa Bingley nodded. "Oh, yes. Quite true."

Will had heard enough. One of them, or perhaps all of them, must have made Elizabeth feel uncomfortable or regret being in their company. He would need to speak with her before retiring for the evening. While listening to Lady Fitzwilliam continue her conversation with Louisa and Caroline, Will reluctantly agreed that Sam's arguments had some merit. None in his family would be happy for Will to marry Elizabeth.

Elizabeth and Jane sat on Elizabeth's bed. Elizabeth looked around the room. Had Miss Graves been correct? Could she ever grow accustomed to a life like this? Lady Fitzwilliam had not been rude to Elizabeth, but she tolerated Caroline's rudeness, which was enough to make Elizabeth desire to avoid their company. Pleading a headache came naturally to her. For as long she could remember, her stepmother had been complaining of headaches. If she ever truly needed to, Elizabeth thought she could even pretend to swoon or have an attack of nerves.

"Are you certain you feel well, Lizzy?" Jane asked Elizabeth in concern.

"I am quite well. I merely detest Caroline Bingley."

Jane's blue eyes rounded. "She is Mr. Charles's sister. She has seemed most friendly to me."

"She is friendly to you, my dear, because you will tolerate her. She also knows no soul in creation could speak a negative word about you. To be the friend of Jane Bennet would mean something in the world." Elizabeth shook her head. "She gains nothing by a false friendship with me."

"Do you really think she is only using me?"

"If she does not enjoy your friendship, she is

far more foolish than I would suppose. However, I do believe she is cunning enough to see there is no benefit to becoming my friend." Elizabeth's lips turned up and formed a wry smile as she reconsidered. "Now that I think about it, she should be grateful for my company. I surely show the world how truly ladylike and accomplished she is by comparison to my own wild behaviour."

Jane giggled. "You are not wild. You...well, you..."

"Go on. I am waiting to hear a compliment in there," Elizabeth laughed.

"You are rusticated!" Jane cried in triumph. "Rustic beauty is all the rage. Now, that is precisely what you are. If others cannot appreciate you as you are, then it would be no different than calling a wildflower a weed merely because it looked out of sorts in a perfectly manicured garden." Jane nodded as though she completely settled the idea.

"That will not work on me," Elizabeth laughed and shook her head. "For people do call wildflowers weeds."

"I never was the great debater."

"It is just as well. Mama says I am far too argumentative, and I will never catch the eye of any man."

"Oh, I think you have."

"What do you mean?" Elizabeth fiddled with a tassel on her blanket.

"Mr. Fitzwilliam could not keep his eyes off you this evening. In fact, he seems to frequently desire to be in your company, or you two go missing together entirely."

"That was merely one time, and we wandered too far in the park. We were hardly alone."

Jane nodded and bit back a smile. "And during the Sardines game?"

"I...I...I..." Elizabeth gulped. "I found a wonderful hiding place but fell asleep and awoke too late to return to the game."

"And you did not see him at all?"

"What are you asking me, Jane?"

"I ask no questions. I merely make observations. I believe that Mr. Fitzwilliam is sweet on you."

"That would seem quite the stretch, for I have no fortune or rank, and hardly any beauty. The heir of Pemberley could certainly attract the notice of any lady."

Jane raised a brow. "Does that mean he is attracted yours?"

"That is not what I meant to say."

"And yet it is exactly what you did say." Jane chuckled and playfully nudged into Elizabeth's shoulder.

"How should a lady act if a gentleman is sweet on her?" Elizabeth fiddled with the tassel on her blanket once more before looking up and searching Jane's face for clues.

"I think most importantly you should not act any differently than you normally would."

Elizabeth nodded. "Yes, I would not want to appear to be trapping him." She sighed and covered her face with her hands. "Jane, I am in so far in over my head!"

"You need not be so mortified," Jane said as she smoothed her fingers through Elizabeth's hair. "Falling in love will happen to all of us."

Elizabeth blushed, and her head immediately popped up to meet Jane's gaze. "How did you know? That is to say...I...oh!"

"It must come as a shock to you, because I think you would much rather have fallen in love with a poor farmer and not until you are fifty than to find yourself helplessly desiring the good opinion of such a young and powerful man."

"Indeed. I cannot fit into his world. This is madness."

"I would not say that. You are both full young, and there is no need to rush into anything. In time, his family and friends will see how happy you make him and will support his choice. You will both learn and grow to fit into your new positions in the world. I do not doubt that my dear Lizzy could be anything she desired, including the next Mrs. Darcy of Pemberley."

Elizabeth cocked her head to one side looked at her sister. "I had never complained about Will's family and friends not supporting me. I think you speak from your own feelings. I have often seen you talking with Mr. Charles." Elizabeth playfully nudged Jane.

"He is the most amiable gentleman I have ever met."

"And that is saying something!"

"Do not tease me so," Jane smiled. "I have not known so very many gentlemen."

"Not from lack of desire on their part, my dear. I've seen more than one fellow become incoherent or flee at the thought of conversing with you or merely being in the presence of your beauty."

"I am sure that is not true." Jane smoothed her gown. "I would hope it is not. I would not wish to frighten anybody."

Elizabeth shook her head. "It would only prove how foolish and unworthy they are. So, tell me about Mr. Charles."

Jane immediately blushed. "There is nothing else to report. He is excessively friendly, but he is to everybody. However, I greatly enjoy his company. I will be sad when the gentlemen leave on the morrow."

"I do not think the impending separation would affect you so much merely because he is a kind gentleman. Do you feel more for him than any other man you have known?"

Slowly, Jane nodded. "The sensations are so new. One minute I am exhilarated and can hardly catch my breath, and the next I am terrified of being laughed at or being made a fool. What if the feelings are not mutual or welcome? I am not blind to his sisters' desires for him. I know I am not rich or important enough for them. More than this, I do not know what he feels."

"I wish I had some advice for you, but I am unable."

"Yes, I should have advice for you, as I am the older sister. I do not know what to say, though.

When I was your age, I had a gangly youth attempting to court me, but he could not speak in my presence. Instead, he would thrust ill designed posies at me when he called at our Aunt and Uncle Gardiner's house. I also had a portly gentleman nearing our father's age attempt to write me poetry. He talked only of news and weather. My heart was in little danger of either them."

"Would they have been suitable matches? Do you ever regret not encouraging them so that you might have a house of your own and children? It may have been the wiser choice."

"I think you have been speaking to Charlotte a bit too much. She is ever prudent and practical but I do not know that it will lead to great happiness in her life. I'd much rather be alone and happy than in the company of others that I might find tiresome."

"But people change so much. Who we find pleasant now we might one day find tiresome. Think of our own parents."

"It is true that sometimes after years of knowing a person they might annoy or differences of opinions of occur. However, I think Mama and Papa would do more for each other now than they would have fifteen years ago."

"I like that," Elizabeth nodded. "I suppose that is part of making a family. I have been missing the girls while we have been away. It has occurred to me that although they are excessively noisy and bothersome when we are all at Longbourn together, I do love them dearly. Perhaps it is the same with our parents."

Jane stifled a yawn. "As you are not ill, I think I had better leave you. Do not forget to pack, my dear. We will be going to the Gardiners' after the gentlemen leave in the morning."

Elizabeth rolled her eyes. "Yes, yes. I am well on my way to finished." She hugged her sister and said good night.

Chapter Seven

The next hour or so passed in solitude. When Elizabeth's mother first passed away, Mr. Bennet quickly remarried. When the new Mrs. Bennet expected her first child, she found it difficult to get the adequate rest she needed with so many other children underfoot. Sam went to a nearby school while Jane and Elizabeth stayed in London with Mrs. Bennet's brother and new bride. The Miss Bingleys had, more than once, mocked them for their address. Although the son of a solicitor, Mr. Gardiner chose to enter a trade and owned warehouses near Cheapside. His residence was on Gracechurch Street. Elizabeth dearly loved her Aunt and Uncle Gardiner and did not care where they lived.

Soon, Elizabeth heard the other occupants of the house returning to the chambers and settling in for the evening. Finally finished with her packing, but unable to sleep, Elizabeth chose a book from her luggage to read. Before too many pages, someone knocked on her door.

"Enter," she called out. She expected to see Jane or perhaps a maid.

Without looking up, Elizabeth heard the door open and close. The shuffling of feet that did not sound like Jane, or any other lady, brought Elizabeth's head up. She started at what she saw. Will was in her bedchamber. Elizabeth blushed and immediately stood.

"Pardon me, I did not mean to surprise you, or intrude." Will stammered and had a hard time meeting her eyes.

"What are you doing here?" Elizabeth glanced toward the bed where her dressing gown lay.

"They said you were ill and I worried about you." Will took another step closer.

Elizabeth smiled. "As you see, I am well. I preferred my own company to some of the other ladies."

"I am sorry to hear that they were unpleasant. Was anyone rude to you?"

"Not particularly. Or at least not more than usual." Elizabeth shrugged. "Why do you ask? You must tell me what happened after Sam pulled you away."

Will gathered Elizabeth's hands and raised each of them to kiss. Elizabeth's heart skipped a beat, and her insides felt like jelly.

"I need to speak with you," Will said. "But

first, I need to kiss you."

Before Elizabeth could reply, Will had gathered her in his strong arms. Thoughts of how scandalous this meeting was immediately left her mind as his lips met hers. She had never known the pleasure found in the arms of a gentleman. She also never would have thought lips could create such sheer joy or sensation. Nor had she ever expected that kissing could involve so much more than the lips.

Will's mouth was everywhere at once, trailing down her neck to her collarbone then back to her lips. His hands ran a frenzied path across her back and up and down her arms. The thin fabric of her night rail brushed against her skin creating goose pimples making the sensation all the more forceful. Elizabeth clung to Will, propping her arms around his neck and kneading her fingers through his hair. Will groaned and tore away from her lips. As their breathing evened, he pressed their foreheads together.

"I will never let you go. I do not care what they say. I belong with you." To further enunciate his feelings, he squeezed her tightly.

"Will, you said they. Has someone else spoken against us? Besides my brother? My father?"

Will let out a low breath. He led Elizabeth to the bed and had her sit there. Then, he let go of her hand and took several steps away. "I cannot touch you and try to explain. I must think rationally. Touching you while you wear only a night rail and we are in your chamber is exceptionally dangerous to my honour right now."

Elizabeth blushed, but secretly thrilled and knowing she could make Will come undone.

"Sam does disapprove of any match between us. However, that was not unexpected. I believe, in time, he will come around to the idea. He did say he has no objection to my character. No one can say I am unable to provide or would not treat you well." Will paused and frowned a moment. "My father also noted my interest in you."

"Yes, Jane asked me about it as well."

"Perhaps it would have been more prudent for me to conceal my affections, but I am glad others can see my obvious admiration for you. I want them to see that you are worthy of my hand."

Elizabeth's heart beat rapidly in her chest. She could hardly credit the words she was hearing. Will had not asked; yet, everything he said indicated he intended marriage.

Pledged

"My father has expressed some concerns." Will began to pace around the room. "Among them was the short nature of our acquaintance, but he says he will support my decision in the end."

Elizabeth nodded. Yes, their short acquaintance was a matter of concern, but she could not deny her heart. She had not known Fitzwilliam Darcy for long, but she knew he would never give her any reason to distrust him or change her opinion of his honour. She had been wrong about him before, due to her insecurities; she would not question him again.

Will stopped in front of Elizabeth and the corners of his mouth tilted up in a light smile. "When I return from my holiday, I could visit Longbourn. There must be a house nearby I could rent, or I could stay at the inn."

"We do have a guest room." Elizabeth smiled at Will. "You are more than welcome to stay with us."

"Oh, in that case," Will grinned, "I thank you for the invitation. I will be sure to take the opportunity of convenience to be very near my intended. After a suitable amount of time, we could announce our engagement. If you do not mind a modest income of five hundred pounds per annum, we might marry within the year."

Elizabeth's hand flew to her heart. "You are speaking of things that require questions, and you have had no answers. I believe you are getting ahead of yourself, sir."

"Allow me to rectify that." Will drop to one knee and took Elizabeth's hands in his. "Marry me, Elizabeth Bennet, not because I am the heir to Pemberley or come from a wealthy family. Marry me because you love me as I love you. Marry me because you see the man I really am. Your support makes me a stronger and better man than I had ever thought I could be. Marry me because I see who you really are and appreciate every nuance. I want to discover every new thing about you every day until I draw my last breath. Marry me because I could search my entire life and never find another lady as worthy as you." Will raised Elizabeth's hands to his mouth.

Elizabeth shook her head and Will immediately stood, taking a step back.

"Pardon me, but I believed you would hear my proposal with enthusiasm. Do you object to something about me or the limited amount of time we have known each other?"

Elizabeth intended to hold back her laughter, but a giggle escaped. "No, not that." She stood and threw her arms around Will. After peppering his face with kisses, she drew back. "I do love you!

As terrified as I am, I will happily be your wife." She paused as Will wrapped his arms around her waist. "I only found it amusing that not once in your well-articulated speech did you make a request. Instead, it was all demands: Marry me, marry me, marry me."

At first, Will looked affronted, but then a smile came to his lips. "I think I will enjoy being teased by you for the rest of my life."

"Even when admonished you still will not ask the question?"

"Oh, I have many questions. How are you so beautiful? How do you fit so perfectly in my arms?" Will nuzzled his head into Elizabeth's hair. "How do you smell so fragrant? How soon can we marry?"

Will scooped Elizabeth into his arms and she giggled. "You are the one who told me we would have to wait for a year."

Will set Elizabeth down gently on the bed and sat next to her. Turning, he stroked her cheek before meeting her lips. When he withdrew, he said, "I already see how my future can be improved with a wife. You are far more intelligent on these matters than I am."

"That is a burden I believe I can bear."

Will wrapped his arms around Elizabeth and kissed her lips once more before bringing her head to rest on his chest. For several minutes, she listened to his heartbeat.

"I offer you my hand in marriage. If I had not one penny to my name, I would still offer it. Would that be enough for you? Will you have me? Will you marry me, sweet, sweet Lizzy?"

Elizabeth smiled against Will's chest and pulled back to meet his eyes. "I would marry you, Fitzwilliam Darcy, if I had a thousand offers from all the richest men in the world. It is you and your heart that I love. I only tremble at being selected by so great a man."

Gathering Elizabeth into his arms, Will pulled her to sit on his lap. Once there, she placed her arms around his neck and leaned into his kiss. Will's hands travelled similar paths as before, up and down Elizabeth's arms and back. Soon, his fingers caressed her shoulders and slipped underneath the fabric of her night rail, causing her to shiver and gasp. Will must have enjoyed the sensation, for his kiss deepened. Next, his lips left hers and descended her throat and across her collarbone. Will pushed the strap of her night rail to the side and he pressed a lingering kiss on the exposed skin.

Elizabeth's heart hammered in her chest and desires she had never known before coursed through her. If Will asked for more intimacy, she would never be able to tell him no. Instead, Will ceased his movements and held Elizabeth to his chest once more.

"Soon, Lizzy. Soon." Will press a kiss into Elizabeth's hair. "I never thought I would find this. I never thought I could combine passion and such deep respect for one woman. I am constantly in awe of you."

"I feel the same way," Elizabeth said. "However, I think you can articulate it better."

The clock in the chamber chimed the hour, and they loosened their hold on one another. Standing, Elizabeth escorted Will to her door. "I think we will have to adjust some of your plans for the future. However, coming to Longbourn and publicly courting me there is a stroke of genius."

"Does that mean I cannot persuade you to smuggle yourself aboard one of our carriages and elope while we are in Scotland?" Will smirked.

Elizabeth quite loved Will's joke. Still, she answered soberly. "We would only choose that route if we felt we had no other option because we were afraid of the consequences of facing certain people's disapproval. I have already told your father and, now, I will tell you, I always rise to every attempt of intimidating me."

"My avenging Goddess," Will said and kissed her forehead. "I agree, we will give our family a chance to come to the idea of our marriage before resorting to such desperate tactics." Will's lips met hers and lingered. "But I vow, I will marry you one day, Elizabeth Bennet. You are imprinted on my heart, and there is room for no other."

Elizabeth sighed as she returned his kiss. "You have my whole heart, Will Darcy. I will never give it to another. I will wait for you. When you return to me, we will plan our future."

Will embraced Elizabeth once more before whispering in her ear. "Fear not, my love. Fitzwilliam Darcy always gets his way, and I will find a way to marry you with the blessing of our families."

Elizabeth nodded as she fervently believed his promise. Opening the door, she made sure the hall was empty before Will left her chamber. She fell asleep that night confident of Will's love and knowing she needed nothing else in life.

To be continued in

Reunited

Coming 2018!

Sample of Reunited

Coming autumn 2018!

Chapter One

September 26, 1811

Sitting at the desk in his London townhouse, Fitzwilliam Darcy's hand shook as he attempted to read Bingley's note. Determined to not display his anxieties, Darcy paced around the room. Finally, he sat in a chair and browsed an agricultural report until his friend arrived.

Ten minutes past his appointed time, the butler announced Bingley's arrival. Darcy stood to greet him.

"Darcy, it has been an age. I was sorry to hear Georgiana felt poorly the whole summer and we could not meet. How does she fare now?"

Darcy managed a small smile as both men sat. "It is always good to see you. My sister is much recovered, thank you. Tell me about this estate you have leased. Hertfordshire, is it?"

Bingley gave Darcy a curious look. "If you know that much, then you have read my note and know it is called Netherfield. You also know it is quite close to Longbourn, which you should recall..."

"Yes, as the Bennet estate." Darcy paused. Tumultuous emotions rioted in his body. As his heart pounded a blistering headache formed. "You cannot blame me for not being able to read through all these blots."

Bingley smiled at the tease. "Will you come and visit? I know your feelings on the Bennets, but it has been five years."

Darcy closed his eyes as painful memories threatened to intrude. Shaking his head to clear the thoughts, he opened his eyes and met Bingley's. "Yes, of course. We must all move forward with our lives."

Bingley gave an ebullient smile and waxed long on the house and its situation. "Louisa and Hurst will come, and Caroline will be my hostess. Will you bring Georgiana?"

Fear and rage temporarily clouded Darcy's vision. Regaining control, he answered, "I...I will leave it to her to determine."

Bingley openly gaped at his friend. "You will allow her to decide?"

Darcy shifted uncomfortably in his seat. "Of course. She is growing older and must have some independence. I cannot order her life forever."

Bingley nodded approvingly, then turned serious. "I have attempted to keep in contact with the Bennets over the years, did I ever tell you?"

Darcy shook his head. "No, you have not. You must have worried about bringing up such a painful subject."

Bingley agreed.

Darcy picked at imaginary lint on his breeches. "What news have you heard?"

"Scarcely a thing. Mr. Bennet only replies around twice a year. In October and then usually in June..." Bingley trailed off for a moment. "They are all quite well."

Darcy smiled a little. "I can imagine he enjoys telling tales of his grandchildren."

Bingley's brow furrowed. "Darcy...all the girls are still at home."

Darcy's head jerked up.

Bingley continued as though he noticed nothing. "I cannot imagine why. I have never met a more angelic creature than Miss Bennet, and Miss Elizabeth was quite pretty as well. The men in Hertfordshire must be blind or stupid." Then he paused, and a solemn look crossed his face. "Or perhaps five years has been slow to heal their pains as well as ours."

Darcy could only nod his head. The two men, now masters of their homes, sat in silence for several minutes.

Bingley stood and clapped a hand on Darcy's shoulder. "I will be escorting Caroline and the others on the Fourteenth after the house is ready for visitors. Will you ride with us then?"

Darcy flinched and then agreed, "Certainly. Apollo could use a good stretch."

The men said their farewells and Bingley departed. Darcy walked back to his desk and picked up Bingley's note again, this time with determination. "It is time."

Acknowledgments

To my author friends Leenie and Zoe that always were willing to hold my hand, nothing can take your place in my heart.

Thank you to the countless other people of the JAFF community who have inspired and encouraged me.

Last but not least, I could never have written, let alone published, without the love and support of my beloved husband and babies!

About the Author

Born in the wrong era, Rose Fairbanks has read nineteenth-century novels since childhood. Although she studied history, her transcript also contains every course in which she could discuss Jane Austen. Never having given up all-nighters for reading, Rose discovered her love for Historical Romance after reading Christi Caldwell's Heart of a Duke Series.

After a financial downturn and her husband's unemployment had threatened her ability to stay at home with their special needs child, Rose began writing the kinds of stories she had loved to read for so many years. Now, a best-selling author of Jane Austen-inspired stories, she also writes Regency Romance, Historical Fiction, Paranormal Romance, and Historical Fantasy.

Having completed a BA in history in 2008, she plans to finish her master's studies someday. When not reading or writing, Rose runs after her two young children, ignores housework, and profusely thanks her husband for doing all the dishes and laundry. She is a member of the Jane Austen Society of North America and Romance Writers of America.

You can connect with Rose on Facebook, Twitter, Instagram, Pinterest, and her blog: http://rosefairbanks.com

To join her email list for information about new releases and any other news, you can sign up here: http://eepurl.com/bmJHjn

Also by Rose Fairbanks

Jane Austen Inspired Fiction

The Gentleman's Impertinent Daughter
Letters from the Heart
Undone Business
No Cause to Repine
A Sense of Obligation
Love Lasts Longest
Once Upon a December
Mr. Darcy's Kindness
Sufficient Encouragement
Renewed Hope
Mr. Darcy's Bluestocking Bride
Extraordinary Devotion
Mr. Darcy's Miracle at Longbourn
Imagining Mr. Darcy
The Secrets of Pemberley

Paranormal Regency

Cinderella's Phantom Prince and Beauty's Mirror Anthology

Made in the USA
Middletown, DE
28 October 2018